The Gh... ...tic

Aunt Clare, wh... ...amily house at Rainbow Falls, offers Amy the chance to escape from the "burden" of sister-sitting. Amy jumps at the chance. She is intrigued by the mystery surrounding the family history and particularly by the beautiful doll's house in the attic. But why should Aunt Clare hate it so? What was so appalling about her grand parents death that makes her refuse to tell Amy what happened?

Only when Louise, Amy's retarded younger sister, comes to stay do the Treloar family find out exactly what happened on that grisly night and Aunt Clare is freed from her guilt at last.

For Beverly Butler Olsen, dear friend,
talented writer, and doll's house-lover, and
for Cherry Barr Jerry, whose marvellous
doll's houses made me want to create an imaginary
one of my own.

The Ghosts in the Attic

Betty Ren Wright

Hippo Books
Scholastic Publications Limited
London

Scholastic Publications Ltd.,
10 Earlham Street, London WC2H 9RX, UK

Scholastic Inc.,
730 Broadway, New York, NY 10003, USA

Scholastic Tab Publications Ltd.,
123 Newkirk Road, Richmond Hill,
Ontario L4C 3G5, Canada

Ashton Scholastic Pty. Ltd.,
P.O. Box 579, Gosford, New South wales,
Australia

Ashton Scholastic Ltd.,
165 Marua Road, Panmure, Auckland 6,
New Zealand

First published in the USA by Holiday House, 1983

First published in the UK by Scholastic Book Services Inc., 1985
Reprinted 1985, 1987

Original title The Dollhouse Murders
Copyright © 1983 by Betty Ren Wright
ISBN 0 590 70347 1

Typeset in Plantin by Gilbert Composing Services, Leighton
Buzzard

Contents

1.

"She Can't Help the Way She Is"

Amy Treloar kicked off her shoes and climbed on to a cushioned bench in the middle of Regents Mall. The mall was crowded with Friday-evening shoppers, some of whom turned to stare.

"Can you see her?" Ellen Kramer asked. "You ought to be able to see her. She's so—"

"Big," Amy finished and hopped down from the bench. It was true; she should have been able to find Louise's bright blue anorak, even in a crowd. At eleven, Louise was five centimetres taller than twelve-year-old Amy, and she weighed ten kilos more. She was the biggest girl in her class at the Stadler School for Exceptional Children.

"My mother is going to kill me," Amy

moaned. "She hangs on to Louise every single minute when they go out shopping together."

"Did she ever wander away before?"

"Only about a million times," Amy said. It was the first time she'd gone shopping with Ellen—the first time they'd planned to do something together after school. Ellen was new in Claiborne, and Amy wanted to have her for a friend. *This'll probably finish it,* Amy thought. *We're wasting the whole afternoon. This'll be the shortest friendship on record.*

"What can we do? Does she know how to make a phone call home?" Ellen was looking at a window display of designer jeans, probably wishing she'd come to the mall alone.

"She gets mixed up," Amy said. "Besides, my mother isn't home yet. Let's go down to the intersection. She might be round the corner where we can't see her."

As they neared the intersection, a squawking sound cut through the piped music. A moment passed before Amy realized that the squawking was voices.

"Oh, no," she groaned. She'd recognized two words: *Louise Treloar.* There was a ripple of childish laughter.

Amy darted ahead. Around the corner, a thick carpet had been laid down the centre of the pavement, and a puppet stage was set up at one end. A crowd of small children and their mothers sat on the carpet and looked up at the stage, where a hawk-nosed puppet was shrieking questions at the audience. In the centre of the group stood Louise, her face

2

shining with excitement. She was answering the puppet in a voice as shrill as his own.

Amy felt rather than saw Ellen step back round the corner. If only she could back away, too! But she couldn't. Already some of the mothers were looking annoyed.

"Louise!" Amy worked her way through the audience, trying not to step on small fingers. "I'm sorry. Excuse me, please." She grasped a sleeve of the blue anorak and tugged. "Come on!"

Louise turned, her broad face radiant. "The puppet talks to me, Amy," she said. "He asks my name."

"Louise, move! This is for little kids." She gripped her sister's wrist. Louise let herself be dragged away, but her eyes didn't leave the stage.

"Bye," she called. "Bye-bye, puppet."

"Bye, sweetie," the puppet replied. "Come back soon." There was laughter and some exasperated sighs from the mothers. "Who else is going to talk to me?" the puppet demanded.

A chorus of little voices sounded behind them as Amy pulled Louise into the main part of the mall. Ellen was several shops away, examining a display of shoes. Her face was carefully blank when they joined her, and she didn't look at Louise at all.

"What shall we do now?" Amy asked quickly. "Do you want to shop for something special, Ellen?"

Ellen shrugged. "We could go to the Casual Shop and look at the sweaters," she said. "If you think it's all right." She risked a hasty glance at Louise.

"I want to see the puppets," Louise said. "Let's go back, Amy. I like the puppets."

"We're going to the Casual Shop," Amy snapped.

"Come on." Louise's mouth opened wide in the beginning of a wail. "It's down this way, past the flower shop," Amy pointed. Her sister loved flowers.

"Where?" Louise broke away and started across the mall.

Amy let her go. There was no reason to hold Louise's hand every minute, as long as she kept her in sight.

"Are you going to buy a sweater?" she asked Ellen. "I wish I could."

"A rugby shirt, maybe. I want a striped one." They walked slowly, following the blue anorak. "I can't buy it, but if I find exactly the right one"—Ellen rolled her eyes and grinned—"I can just sort of mention it at home. My birthday's in two weeks time."

"Two weeks? Mine is next Friday—June the fifteenth. The last day of school."

"Mine's the twenty-second. We're practically twins."

"Maybe we can have a party or something to celebrate," Amy suggested. "A double birthday party would be fun."

She waited for an answer, but Ellen was looking at the flower shop, where Louise had stopped to gaze at the display. "Oh-oh," she said. "That man . . . "

4

Amy followed her stare. A tall man had come out of the shop and was shaking his finger in Louise's face. Louise shrank back and looked round for help.

Amy started to run. This time Ellen followed right behind her.

"—and don't ever do that again!" the man shouted as the girls drew close. "You shouldn't be running around alone—" He stopped as Amy reached for Louise's hand. "Are you with her?"

Amy nodded. The hand in hers was trembling.

"Then why don't you watch her?" He was furious. "Look what she's done!"

A cluster of yellow tulips in pots stood on a low shelf in front of the shop window. One of the blooms was broken and drooped over the edge of its pot.

"That's an expensive plant ruined!" the man fumed. "I ought to make your parents pay for it. They shouldn't let this child out without someone responsible enough to look after her."

Amy's face burned. "I'm sorry," she said over Louise's mounting sobs. "We have tulips at home, and she knows it's okay to pick *them*. She just forgot—I mean, she understands she shouldn't pick other people's flowers, but she likes them so much—"

"That helps a lot, doesn't it?" the florist said sarcastically. "Somebody'd better teach her how to behave if she's going to wander round in a public place."

Amy's embarrassment was swallowed up in rage. She had five pounds in her wallet, the last of her Christmas money from her grandmother. She'd hoped to find a swimsuit today and use the five pounds to put down as a deposit on it until after her birthday. Suddenly, though, it was more important to make this man regret his rudeness.

"I'll pay for the plant," she said. "Louise, stop crying. It's all right." She glared at the florist. "How much is it?"

He glared back. Then his gaze flicked over the people who had stopped to listen and were looking at Louise.

"That poor child," one woman said. "She's heart-broken. Look how she's crying. She didn't know any better, you can tell."

Amy took the five-pound note from her wallet and held it out. "I'll need change," she said.

Louise stopped crying. The mall became very quiet. The florist started to reach for the note, then turned away in disgust.

"Forget it," he snapped. "Just keep that girl away from my stock." He went back into the shop, muttering under his breath.

The mall came back to life. Spectators moved off, shaking their heads, and the three girls were left by themselves.

"Let's get away from here," Amy said. "I hate that man! If I were a tulip, I'd fall over and die just having him around."

"Die?" Louise looked down at the bright yellow flowers. She was ready to cry again. "Flowers die?"

"No, no, no! Not unless you pick them!"

"Maybe we'd better just go home," Ellen said. "I don't think I feel like shopping today."

Amy felt sick. "Okay," she said. "Whatever you want." *It was awful,* Ellen would tell her mother when she got home. *Everybody was looking at us. I'll never go shopping with Amy Treloar again.*

Outside, the sun was low in the sky. An early-evening breeze stirred the flags across the mall's main entrance. Louise lagged a bit behind Amy and Ellen. "The puppet show . . ." she murmured sadly as they started across the car park. Amy pretended not to hear. She was waiting for Ellen to say something.

"You were fantastic in there, Amy. I loved it when you pulled out the money. I was scared to death of that man. What a beast!"

Amy took a deep breath. Maybe Ellen wasn't completely disgusted after all. "I was scared, too," she confessed. "But he made me so angry! Louise makes me angry too, but I still don't like it when people insult her. She can't help the way she is."

That was something Amy kept telling herself. Lately, though, it hadn't helped much. The only time she could feel sympathy for her sister was when someone else spoke sharply to Louise or made fun of her. Otherwise, resentment was always boiling under the surface.

"I'm sorry Louise spoiled the shopping," Amy hurried on. "I didn't want to bring her with us, but my mother's at work, and there's no one at home after school."

"It's hard for you," Ellen said. "I don't know

if I could do it."

"You would if you had to." The words came out tartly, and Amy rushed to change the subject. "About the picnic tomorrow," she said. "What time should I pick you up?"

She stressed the *I* ever so slightly, hoping Ellen would take that as a signal that Louise wouldn't be coming. The two girls had made plans for Saturday earlier in the week, when Amy had mentioned Rainbow Falls north of the town, and Ellen had said she'd like to see it. Since they'd be taking their bikes, there was no question of Louise tagging along. She couldn't ride a bike, though she'd tried at least a hundred times.

"Oh, I meant to tell you," Ellen said, "I can't go tomorrow. My uncle and aunt are coming from Chicago for the day, and my mother wants me to stay at home." She ignored Amy's tiny gasp of dismay. "We hardly ever see them. I'm sorry—maybe we can have the picnic later."

"Of course." Amy thought of the yellow tulip hanging over the edge of the pot. That was how she felt inside—broken. Dead! A few minutes ago Ellen had seemed to understand what it was like to have Louise for a sister. But she wasn't really any different from the other girls who were too busy to do things with Amy when they found out Louise might be there, too. People were all the same.

They walked in silence to the corner where Ellen had to turn off. "I'm really sorry about tomorrow," she said.

Amy felt as if her face might crack when she

spoke. "Have fun with you aunt and uncle. I'll see you on Monday."

"Right." Ellen hurried away.

Amy took Louise's hand and waited for the light to change. Her sister's face was puffy and streaked with dried tears, but she looked around cheerfully at the busy street. "Tomorrow we can see the puppets again," she said.

"No way!" The toot of a car horn cut through Amy's reply. It was their mother, on her way home from work. She waved and pointed to the opposite corner. Amy led Louise across the street, and they climbed into the front seat of the car. Amy was squeezed between the door and Louise's soft bulk.

"Well, did you find the swimsuit you wanted?" Mrs. Treloar asked. And then, without waiting for an answer, "What's the matter, Louise? Have you been crying?"

Louise nodded.

"Well, what happened, Amy? Did somebody say something nasty to her?"

"The florist in the mall," Amy replied. "She tried to pick a tulip from a pot, and he made a big scene."

Louise rubbed her eyes with her fists.

"And where were *you* when it happened?" Mrs. Treloar demanded. She sounded tired. "You certainly couldn't have been watching her very closely if she had a chance to—"

"I can't watch her every second!"

Mrs. Treloar's lips tightened. "Don't be impudent," she said. "We trust you, Amy. Louise trusts you. She needs your protection."

Afterwards, it seemed to Amy that a whole volcano of anger exploded inside her right then. She'd heard those words many times before. This time, the anger couldn't be held back.

"I don't want her to need me!" she shouted. "I'm sick of baby-sitting and losing my friends and having everybody stare when we go past. I don't want to protect her any more. I'm never, going to take her anywhere again!"

Mrs. Treloar's hands on the steering wheel were rigid. "I can't believe what I just heard," she said. "I can't believe you can be so cruel. So selfish! A girl who has everything—"

"I don't have *anything*," Amy roared. "You want me to drag her around behind me the rest of my life. Well, I won't do it!"

She had her hand on the door handle, ready to jump out the minute the car pulled into the drive. She had to get away—away from Louise and from her mother and from the terrible things she'd heard herself saying. She wanted to run and not stop.

"You can be sure your father will hear about this when he gets home." Mrs. Treloar said. "I'm going to tell him every word of this conversation. He'll be as ashamed of you as I am." She slammed on the brakes, millimetres from the garage door.

Amy leaped out, and Louise tumbled after her. "Wait for me," she shouted. "Wait for me."

"Louise, you stay here," Mrs. Treloar ordered. "Come inside, and we'll have some biscuits. Let Amy go. She's behaving very badly."

With her hands over her ears, Amy tore down the street. *Biscuits!* she thought. *Let Amy go!* She turned the corner, trying not to hear the plaintive cry that followed her.

"Tomorrow, Amy. The puppet show. Don't forget, Amy. You must take me!"

2.

"The Most Perfect Doll's House"

The sign said RAINBOW FALLS 3. Amy's
run had long since slowed to a walk, now she
hesitated, aware that darkness was closing in
and she was leaving Claiborne behind her. Her
eyes burned and her chest felt tight, but mostly
she was just tired. Somewhere back there she'd
shed much of her anger in a storm of tears.

Ahead, lights glimmered in far-apart houses.
Misty patches of dark loomed between them.
It's pitiful, she thought, *being out here all alone in
the cold with no one to care, while other people are
snug and safe with their families.*

Well, actually the June evening was pleasantly
warm, not cold. And if her parents didn't know
where she was and maybe didn't care, there was
someone nearby who did. She knew that Aunt

Clare, her father's sister, would be glad to see her.

Aunt Clare was staying temporarily in the huge old house that had belonged to Amy's great-grandparents. She had invited Amy to drop in anytime, but so far, Amy hadn't done it. She felt shy with this aunt, who had lived in Chicago since long before Amy was born. The two evenings she'd spent with the Treloars since her return to Claiborne had been uncomfortable. She and Amy's mother seemed to have little to say to each other.

But Aunt Clare likes me, Amy told herself. *She said she thought we were a lot alike. I'll just stay for a little while, and then I'll go home.* Maybe Aunt Clare would give her a lift.

At the next crossroads Amy turned, then turned again on to a narrow gravel road lined with tall weeds and an occasional oak. The road seemed longer in the twilight than it had during the daylight visits to the house she'd made with her father. Amy walked faster, looking for the sharp curve that led into the garden. Night settled round her, rustling with the sounds of small creatures in the undergrowth. Her heart sank at the sudden thought that Aunt Clare might have gone into town for the evening.

Then the house loomed in front of her, with lights shining out from every floor. Even the attic was lit. Amy had never seen the house look so friendly. When she'd come with her father, before Aunt Clare's return, they'd usually stayed outside, walking around to look at doors and windows. On the few occasions when they'd gone in to check the heating and the water pipes, they'd remained only a few minutes, tiptoeing like burglars through the rooms full of musty furniture.

Amy climbed the wide front steps and crossed the porch. The wrought-iron knocker, shaped like an eagle, thunked hollowly against the front door. Aunt Clare didn't answer. Amy knocked again, then tried the handle. The door was unlocked. She let herself in and stood uncertainly in the hall. The house was very quiet.

"Aunt Clare?" Her voice sounded peculiar—almost like a wail—in the stillness. "Is anybody here?"

There was a rush of footsteps on a bare floor overhead, then a pause.

"Who—who's down there?" Aunt Clare sounded far away and a little scared.

"It's me—Amy."

"Good grief, Amy! Oh, I'm glad it's just you. I mean, I couldn't imagine . . . Come right on up here."

The curving staircase rose through a tower at one side of the hall. Amy ran up to the second floor and looked along the broad corridor. Near its end, the door to the attic stood open.

"Keep coming," Aunt Clare called. "I'm up here in the storehouse of the world."

Amy ran down the hall and up the attic steps. Aunt Clare waited at the top, dressed in jeans and a pink shirt knotted at the waist. Her grey-streaked hair was tied back under a rose-coloured scarf, and her thin face was bright with welcome. She threw her arms round Amy and hugged her.

"Whew! You can't imagine how my heart's thudding! It's a real shock to hear another human voice in this old tomb!"

Amy hugged her back. "I'm sorry I scared you," she said. "The door was unlocked—"

"And a good thing, too," her aunt interrupted. "Though I thought it was locked. I never would have heard the knocker up here." She glanced down the stairs. "Did someone come with you? You didn't come all this way by yourself, did you?"

Amy nodded and backed away from Aunt Clare's probing look. "What are you doing up here—looking for something?"

"Looking for things to throw away," Aunt Clare replied. "And finding them. Tonnes of things! I'll have to hire a lorry to carry them off. Moth-eaten clothes, broken chairs, cracked mirrors . . . ." Amy could feel the concerned look that followed her as she wandered round the attic.

"How about a Coke?" Aunt Clare suggested. "I have to get away from all the dust anyway—I think I'm allergic to it. Or to work, I'm not sure which." She sneezed as if to prove it.

Amy was in a far corner of the attic. "Okay," she agreed. But she didn't move, because directly in front of her was a mysterious sheeted object that came to a peak at one corner. The thing—whatever it was—was almost as tall as Amy. She leaned forward and gave the sheet a tug. Dust rose around her as the cover slipped to the floor.

"Oh." Amy gave a squeaky little gasp. "Oh, Aunt Clare, look at this. It's the most perfect doll's house I've ever seen." She dropped to her knees as her aunt came to stand beside her. "*It's this house!* Look! Here's the stair tower, and the front porch, and the eagle door-knocker—everything! It's just beautiful."

Aunt Clare ran her finger along one side of the facade. The entire front of the house swung away, revealing rooms full of furniture.

Amy loved miniatures. Some of the bookshelves in her bedroom at home had been emptied to make room for tiny tables, lamps, a chest of drawers, even a piano, that she'd bought with her own money or that had been given to her. The whole unhappy afternoon—Louise, Ellen, the scene with her mother—all was forgotten as she stared at the exquisitely detailed rooms.

"There's the grandfather clock," she marvelled. "It has a ship painted on it, just like the real one in the hall downstairs. And the rugs are the same. And the painting above the fireplace. And look at the tiny candlesticks!"

"There used to be a pair just like them on the dining-room table downstairs," Aunt Clare said. "Every detail is correct." Her voice was curiously flat.

"Where did it come from?" Amy demanded. "Was it yours when you were a little girl?" She thought about the times she'd come to the old house with her father and had waited impatiently for him to say they could leave. If she'd known the doll's house was here, she would have wanted to stay all day.

"It was my fifteenth birthday present from Grandma and Grandpa Treloar—your great-grandparents," Aunt Clare said. "Can you imagine giving a fifteen-year-old a doll's house?"

"I'd love it," Amy said. "I'll love miniatures all my life." Maybe she and Aunt Clare weren't so much alike after all. "I could sit and look at it for hours."

"Well," Aunt Clare said, "Grandma and Grandpa expected me to *play* with it. It was an expensive, beautiful reminder that they wanted a little girl in their house, not a teenager who was in a hurry to grow up." Her voice softened as she reached in and picked up a tiny needlepoint pillow from the sofa in the parlour. "Grandma Treloar made a lot of the furnishings herself. It was a lovely gift—I know that. And I was a wicked, ungrateful girl. Do you know, I cried when I saw it? I'd been hoping for a record player."

Amy couldn't imagine being disappointed with such a gift. "Which bedroom was yours?" she asked.

Her aunt pointed to a corner room. "It's the only one that isn't perfectly reproduced to the last detail," she said with a wry little smile. "I had Elvis Presley posters all over the walls. Grandma Treloar wouldn't go *that* far to be accurate. She made it look the way she thought a young girl's room should be."

Amy examined the canopied bed, the flowered

quilt, the white-painted furniture and ruffled curtains. It was a room for a princess. How could Aunt Clare not have loved it?

"The whole thing was a mistake," Aunt Clare said, as if she could read Amy's thoughts. "I mean, our coming to live here was all wrong. When our parents died, about a week apart—they were on holiday in South America and caught some vicious 'flu bug—I was fourteen and your father was just one year old. A cousin with a big family of his own offered to take Paul and me. We should have gone to them then. But Grandma and Grandpa Treloar wouldn't hear of it. They had lots of room, plenty of money to hire part-time help, and not enough to think about. Grandma's arthritis made her quite lame, and she was terribly afraid of becoming an invalid. I think she hoped your father and I would keep them young. But we were a much bigger job than she'd expected. Especially me." Aunt Clare grimaced at the memory. "We had our first battle the day we moved in. She'd bought a whole wardrobe of ruffly dresses for me to wear to school. When everyone else was wearing pleated skirts and loafers! I had a fit."

Abruptly, Aunt Clare swung shut the hinged front of the house, closing it with a snap. "Oh, well!" She sighed. "It's no use looking back. Let's go downstairs and find something cold to drink before I get thoroughly depressed." She turned and walked swiftly to the top of the stairs. "Coming?"

Reluctantly, Amy stood up. She hated to leave

the doll's house but now that she knew it was there, she intended to come back again. She wanted to examine every piece of furniture, peer into every corner. Finding it seemed a good sign, like finding a four-leaf clover on a day that had brought nothing but trouble.

3.

"So We All Have Problems"

Downstairs in the big kitchen, Aunt Clare set glasses on the table and filled them with ice cubes and cold tea.

"I thought I had Coke, but I haven't," she apologised. "I run out of things all the time. In Chicago—" she paused, her expression wistful—"there was a great little corner shop. I used to shop practically every night on my way home from work." She sipped the iced tea. "It was a friendly street—I loved it."

"Why did you leave?" Amy thought she knew, but she asked anyway. It was nice having a conversation with a grown-up who treated her like an adult.

"I lost my job," Aunt Clare said bluntly. "No job, no money to pay the rent. This house had been empty for four years, ever since Uncle James—your great-uncle—died. He was a real hermit—lived in the kitchen and one bedroom and never touched the rest of the house. He didn't take care of the place, but we were glad to have him move in when. . . when the rest of us left, thirty years ago. After his death, Paul —your father—kept asking me to come back and clear out the house; he didn't know what to do with everything. And this seemed like a good time to do the job." She looked around the kitchen. "Not the cheeriest place to spend a few months, I can assure you, but it'll do for a while." She shook her head. "So we all have problems. What about you, Amy? If you don't mind my saying so, those pretty brown eyes look a bit troubled right now."

Amy hesitated. She hadn't planned to talk about the angry scene that had sent her running out into the countryside.

"You'll think I'm a rat," she said.

"I doubt it. I've done enough ratty things to know how bad it feels. I'm not likely to judge anyone else harshly."

"Amy clutched her glass in both hands. "It's Louise," she said, the words spilling out fast. "I'm so sick of looking after her and smoothing things over when she gets into trouble—and losing friends because of her! That's what happened this afternoon. I know she can't help being brain-damaged. She's like a little kid, and she always will be. I'm just tired of having to think about it. And my mum says I'm really terrible. She says I'm lucky to be the normal one, and I should stop complaining."

Aunt Clare looked thoughtful. "I can imagine her feeling that way. What does your father say?"

Amy shrugged. "Nothing, usually." She searched for words that would describe her father's attitude. "He just wants peace, I suppose," she said. "My mum yells and tells me off, and Dad says, 'Well, well, I'm sure Amy didn't mean it'—whatever *it* is—and he changes the subject. Or he says, 'Let's remember we're a family.' And that's not fair, because I'm the one who has to do all the remembering. Louise just goes on being herself and having her own way."

"Family means a lot to your father," Aunt Clare murmured. "He had so little of it."

"He had you. And Great-Grandma and Great-Grandpa Treloar."

Aunt Clare fluttered her fingers, brushing away the words. "Our parents died when Paul was practically a baby, and we only lived with Grandma and Grandpa Treloar until he was five and I was eighteen. Then they were killed—in an accident—and the cousin who'd wanted to adopt us in the first place took Paul. The poor little boy must have been thoroughly confused by that time. He lost me then, too, because I went to Chicago to look for a job."

Amy tried to picture her tall father as a frightened five-year-old and failed. "That's what I'm going to do," she said. "The minute I'm eighteen. I'm going to get away from Claiborne. I'm going to have a flat and lots of friends and a good job."

"Doing what?" Aunt Clare smiled. "It isn't as simple as it was when I did it. Now they ask which college you went to or which business school trained you."

"Then I'll go to college," Amy vowed. "I'll go anywhere, just as long as it's away from here."

Aunt Clare reached across the table and patted her hand. "You do sound as if you've had your fill of sister-sitting." She seemed to be turning over something in her mind. "I have a suggestion," she said. "And that's all it is—a suggestion. Your mother and father will have to approve. But maybe you and Louise ought to have a break from each other for a while. If you'd like to keep me company for a couple of weeks, I'd love to have you."

The offer took Amy completely by surprise. "Mum wouldn't let me," she said after a moment. "I have to take care of Louise every day until she gets home from work. And when they go out." She couldn't say the rest of what she was thinking—that her mother wouldn't agree because she didn't particularly like Aunt Clare.

"I'll talk to your father first," Aunt Clare said, as if she were a mind reader. "Will he be home by now?"

Amy glanced at her watch and shifted uneasily. Not only would her father be home, but by this time both her parents would be upset by her absence. She could pretend, when she was angry, that they didn't care what she did, but she knew it wasn't true. They wanted to know where she was after dark.

"I'd better call right away," Amy muttered. "He's home, all right, and he's probably furious with me."

Aunt Clare put out a restraining hand. "Let me," she said. She jumped up and hurried down the hall to the telephone niche next to the sitting-room.

Amy waited, hardly knowing what to feel. The harshly lit kitchen was faintly shabby with age. The curtains were thin and yellowed, and the linoleum was faded. There was an ancient gas stove with a high oven at one side, and a refrigerator that thrummed. The sink was small and not quite level; a single shelf above it was crowded with cleaning materials. The whole room was as different from her mother's sparkling, efficient kitchen as it possibly could be.

Amy felt a flicker of homesickness. Could she really leave her family, her bedroom, everything that she knew, and move out to this isolated old house?

It's a sad place, she thought, remembering Aunt Clare's expression when she talked about the past. *I can feel sadness in the air.* But then she thought about the picnic Ellen had called off after Louise got into trouble at the mall. She thought about how her sister would beg to go back to the puppet show tomorrow, and how angry Mum would be if Amy refused to take her.

The voice in the hall sounded warm, smooth, persuasive. Suddenly, Amy was praying that Aunt Clare would be able to make her parents agree to the visit. She wanted to come! In addition to her other reasons, there was the doll's house up in the attic. *I'll dust it and polish the furniture and make it look just like new,* Amy thought. She was picturing the grandfather clock with its tiny gold pendulum and weights, when her aunt came back to the kitchen.

"Well, I've done my best," she said briskly. "Your father wouldn't say yes—I gather your mother is very upset about what happened this afternoon. But he didn't say no, either. I think he wants you to come, Amy, and I'm sure he's going to see what he can do. Of course, they'll have to find a sitter to watch Louise after school for a week or so." She looked thoughtful. 'It'll all take some doing. When you talk to them about it, remember you're invited because I need company. Don't mention Louise at all."

Suddenly Aunt Clare pulled Amy to her feet and swung her around the kitchen. "We could have a terrific time, kiddo! Doesn't it sound like fun!"

"Oh, yes!" Amy flew across the room and collapsed into a rocking chair. Her head whirled. This was just exactly what she wanted, wasn't it? A chance to get away from Louise for while. Of course it was!

But she didn't believe it would happen. Her mother would never let her do it.

4.

"We Love You Very Much, You Know"

"I don't understand why Clare is so lonely all of a sudden," Mrs. Treloar said for the third time since they'd sat down to breakfast. "She talks about the importance of being independent—what's happened to all that independence I'd like to know? She's a very changeable person."

Amy fished for the last banana slice in her cereal bowl and said nothing. She'd heard her parents talking until very late. Maybe they'd talked all night!

"It's possible to be independent and lonely at the same time." Mr. Treloar sounded tired and grumpy. "That house *is* a lonely place, you know. And it's full of very painful memories. I can understand Clare wanting company for a while."

Painful memories? Amy wondered what he meant. She waited for her father to say more about that, but he said, "Staying there will be a nice change for Amy, too."

"Change?" Mrs. Treloar jumped on the word. "Why does a twelve-year-old girl need a change? I think Clare is interfering in something that's none of her business, just because Amy went running out there when she was upset. Now Louise is going to feel abandoned—"

Mr. Treloar looked unhappy. "I don't think Louise is going to feel abandoned," he said. "Not if she has some adventures of her own." He smiled at Louise who had been silent ever since she learned that Amy had been invited to Aunt Clare's. "We're going to ask Mrs. Peck if you can stay with her after school, until Mum gets home from work. You'll have fun."

"No, I won't," Louise said. "I want to go to Aunt Clare's with Amy. I hate Mrs Peck."

Amy's father stood up. "You've stayed with Mrs. Peck before, and you've never said you hated her. I'm going to call her now." He looked at Amy's mother. "Unless you want to do it."

Mrs. Treloar shook her head.

"But if Mrs. Peck agrees, you *will* let Amy go," he insisted. "Just until school's finished?"

Amy's mother looked from him to Amy, who was holding her breath. "If it's so important, I won't stand in the way. But I won't pretend to like the idea. And if it doesn't work out. . . ."

Mr. Treloar went to the study to telephone. Amy glanced uneasily at her mother, and at

Louise, who was rolling her napkin into a tight ball. The kitchen was silent until Mr. Treloar returned.

"All set," he said. "Mrs. Peck is happy to have Louise. You go ahead and pack, Amy, and I'll take you over to Clare's when you're ready."

Louise's wail followed Amy out of the kitchen. "I want to go with Amy! I have to, Mum. I have to."

In the upstairs hallway Amy stopped for a moment, listening to her mother's soothing murmur. Then she went into her bedroom and closed the door.

Her duffel bag was at the back of the wardrobe. She pulled it out and began stuffing it with shoes, jeans, socks, underwear, and pyjamas. A half-dozen blouses and a cotton skirt went in on top, and her hair dryer, shampoo, and toothbrush went into her shoulder bag. She was ready. She wanted to go right away, before the argument began once more.

The telephone rang, and Amy heard Louise run, heavy footed, to answer it.

"Amy, TELEPHONE!"

If only she wouldn't bellow! Amy raced downstairs, wondering if Aunt Clare had changed her mind.

"Hi, it's me. Ellen."

Ellen! Amy hadn't expected to hear from her again.

"My mother's taking my aunt and uncle to visit some friends later this afternoon. I know it'll be too late for a picnic, but maybe you can come over for a couple of hours. We can make brownies or something. If you don't have anything else to do, that is."

Like taking care of Louise. Ellen hadn't said the words, but Amy knew what she meant.

"My mum doesn't usually like me to have friends over when she's out, but she said *one* friend would be all right," Ellen went on. Another pause. She might as well have said it right out—*Retarded sister not wanted.*

Amy pushed down the resentment. She shouldn't blame Ellen for feeling the way she felt herself.

"The thing is, I'm going to stay with my aunt for a while," Amy said. "It's on the way to Rainbow Falls—north of town. I'm leaving in a few minutes." She had an idea and decided to take a chance that Aunt Clare would welcome a second visitor. "Why don't you cycle out there?" she suggested. "I found something terrific in the attic last night—wait till you see it!"

Ellen agreed at once. "You mean you're going to live with your aunt? Just you?"

"I'm only staying a few days."

The girls talked a couple of minutes more, and Ellen promised to be out at Aunt Clare's around three. When Amy put down the phone and turned round, she jumped. Louise was right behind her. Her feet were planted far apart, and her flushed face showed anger and hurt.

"What's terrific, Amy?" she demanded. "What's terrific at Aunt Clare's?"

"Nothing." Amy ducked around her sister and ran back upstairs. She didn't want to look into those accusing eyes. She didn't want to think about how much Louise would love the doll's house.

She'll see it someday. But not now. This is going to be my private time.

Minutes later, as she was about to close her bag, Louise opened the bedroom door and walked in. She carried a vase she'd made at school.

"Here." She laid the vase on the bed. "For your bedroom at that place," she said.

The vase was an olive jar, covered with silver paint and pasted-on pictures of roses. It was one of Louise's dearest treasures.

"You don't want me to take that," Amy protested. "It belongs on your dressing table."

"Take it." Louise stalked out of the room but glanced over her shoulder. "Bring it back when you come home."

"Oh, I will," Amy said. "Thanks a lot." She nestled the vase into the clothes in the duffel bag so it couldn't be broken. "You're going to have a great time at Mrs Peck's," she called. "You'll see."

The only answer was the sound of scrunching springs as Louise threw herself across her bed.

Amy did up the duffel bag and picked up her shoulder bag. She hurried downstairs and out of the front door. Her father was cutting the grass, but he shut off the mower when he saw her coming.

"Can we go right now, Dad?"

"This minute?" He smiled. "All right. Put your bike into the car boot and we'll go. Have you said goodbye to your mother?"

"I will."

She brought her bike from the garage and then went back into the house. Her mother was at the kitchen table, reading a book of Italian recipes and drinking coffee. She always read recipe books when she was upset.

"I'll call you later." Amy bent and kissed her mother's cheek. "Dad's taking me out to Aunt Clare's now."

Mrs. Treloar nodded. "I still don't understand," she said. "I don't see why you're so eager to get away from us. We had a disagreement yesterday, but. . ." She looked up.

Amy moved towards the door. "It's not that I want to get away from you." *Not exactly, anyway.*

"We love you very much, you know."

"I know."

"Louise loves you, too."

"I know." Amy was sure she'd scream if her mother said one more word. "I'll call tomorrow. Goodbye, Mum."

She ran out of the back door and down the steps, almost stumbling in her haste. Her father was in the car, waiting. She slid in on the passenger's side with a sigh of relief.

"All set?" He backed down the driveway.

"All set." If those words meant "Do you feel great about leaving?" she wasn't set at all. But if they meant "Do you want to go?" then she was all set indeed.

5.

"Dolls Can't Move by Themselves"

"This is my room," Amy announced. She led
Ellen into the large corner bedroom Aunt Clare
had prepared for her. The fragrance of lemon oil
and the breeze blowing in from the fields almost
hid the musty smell of the dark red carpet.

"My aunt had to throw away the quilt that was
on the bed," Amy said. "It was full of moths."
She swung open the doors of a gigantic
wardrobe in one corner. "How's this for a great
wardrobe?"

"I love it!" Ellen went to a window and looked
out. "It's really funny not seeing neighbours,"
she said. "I've never been in a country house
before." Amy joined her just as Aunt Clare
came out of the back door with a rubbish bag
and crossed the garden. The cover of the

dustbin next to the garage was tight, and they watched her struggle with it for a moment.

"The covers have to fit well because of the raccoons," Amy said, repeating a detail Aunt Clare had mentioned during lunch. "They come almost every night and try to get at the rubbish."

"Now the attic," Amy said. "I've been saving the best for last. Wait till you see what's up there. Guess!"

"Bats and spiders," Ellen said. "Why don't you just tell me about it?" But she followed willingly enough as Amy led the way back down the hall and switched on the attic light. The stairs creaked as they climbed them, side by side.

At the top, Ellen stopped and looked around at the clutter stacked in front of the dusty, gabled windows. "This could be the set for a spooky film," she commented, but Amy hardly heard her. She ran across the attic, pulling her friend behind her.

"Look!" She pointed at the doll's house in the corner. "What do you think of that?"

Ellen was as stunned as Amy had been the evening before. "Oh, Amy," she breathed. "Look at—at the tiny railings on the porch, and the curtains, and the little curvy pieces above the windows. It's perfect!"

"It's this house," Amy said. "Watch." She ran her fingers down the side until she found the clasp that held the façade in place. There was a small click, and the treasures inside were revealed.

"Wow!" Ellen didn't know what to look at first. She pointed at the little organ in the front sitting-room and then at the wardrobe in the corner bedroom. "And the dining-room chairs!" she exclaimed. "Each one has its own needlepoint cover."

Amy used a fingernail to open the sideboard in the dining-room, and both girls gasped at the sight of tiny dishes and silver pieces stacked on the shelves inside.

"Look at that teapot!"

"Sugar tongs!"

"Amy, these salt and pepper shakers are incredible. They're so tiny, they look like they might disappear."

For half of an hour the girls crouched in front of the house. Finally Ellen leaned back with a sigh. "Your aunt must have loved this," she said. "I wonder if there were any dolls with the house when she got it. That's the only thing that's missing."

Amy looked around. On the floor beside the house was a small wooden box with a landscape painted on it. She lifted the lid. Inside, lying in a row, were four dolls, the tallest about sixteen centimetres high. The man wore a black suit; he had a white moustache, and tiny rimless spectacles were on his nose. The woman was in blue silk, her grey hair drawn up on top of her head in a bun. The other two dolls were a young girl with long brown hair, wearing a dress of palest pink, and a tiny boy in a blue sailor suit.

"Here they are," Amy said. "This must be Grandma and Grandpa Treloar, and here's

Aunt Clare when she was fifteen." She picked up the boy doll. "And this is my father," she said. "Look, Ellen, the arms and legs are jointed, and the hair is real. Did you ever see such perfect little dolls?"

"Never," Ellen sighed. "The Aunt Clare doll looks a bit like you, Amy."

She and Amy picked up the dolls, one by one, and put them on the dining-room chairs, bending the delicate limbs so that the figures sat primly at the table. Then they took tiny dishes from the sideboard and set a place in front of each doll. They were concentrating so hard that they didn't hear Aunt Clare come up behind them.

"The girl doll should be up in her bedroom," she said.

Amy's hand jerked, knocking the grandfather off his chair.

"She was usually sent to her room for impertinence about halfway through dinner, as I remember."

"Every night?" Amy asked, amazed.

Aunt Clare shrugged. "I don't suppose it was every night. It just seems that way now. Come on, haven't you seen enough of this old thing by now? I've made some fudge, if anybody's interested!"

"We're interested." Amy put the grandfather doll back at the table with his family, and Ellen straightened the tiny candlesticks.

"I didn't know there were dolls to go with the house," Amy said. "Grandma Treloar thought of everything, didn't she?"

"Yes she did." Aunt Clare was already at the top of the stairs. "Coming?"

Amy noticed how her aunt's voice changed when she spoke of the doll's house. She sounded as if she were angry but wanted to hide it. It would be better to talk about something else, she decided. She tried to catch Ellen's eye, but her friend was chattering excitedly as she followed Aunt Clare down the attic stairs.

"I wish someone would make a doll that looked like me," she said. "And a house that looked like our house. I'd keep it forever—right in my living room."

"No, you wouldn't," Aunt Clare said. "If it made you unhappy, you'd try to forget it existed—which is, frankly, what I'd like to do. Please." Her smile didn't quite take the sting out of the words. "Now, how about some biscuits with that fudge? I did some baking this morning, in honour of my guest."

"We'd better wash first," Amy said. She grabbed Ellen's hand and led her down the hall to the bathroom, while Aunt Clare continued to the first floor.

"Is something the matter with your aunt?" Ellen demanded, when the door closed behind them. "She sounded angry all of a sudden."

"I don't know," Amy said. "My mum says she's a changeable person, but she's really nice. There's just something about the doll's house that makes her really jumpy. I'm not going to mention it again. I told you—she thinks it was a babyish gift for a fifteen-year-old."

"Well, I think it was a wonderful gift," Ellen

said. "Anybody who doesn't think so is—" She didn't finish the sentence.

Amy wanted to defend her aunt, but secretly she agreed with Ellen. After so many years had passed, you'd think Aunt Clare could forgive her grandparents for giving her a doll's house instead of a record player.

"I have to go back to the attic," Amy said suddenly. "I left the house standing open."

"What's the difference?" Ellen pulled her hair back like the Clare doll's and looked at herself in the mirror.

"The furniture will get dusty. All those rugs and teeny pillows and lace curtains." She washed her hands and dried them. "You go on downstairs. I'll be with you in a minute." She grinned at Ellen's doubtful expression. "Aunt Clare doesn't bite," she said. "She's great—just don't talk about the doll's house. And don't start eating the fudge until I get there."

Before Ellen could argue, Amy left the bathroom and hurried back to the attic stairs. She flicked the switch that lit the overhanging bulb at the top. As she climbed, she found herself walking on tiptoe. The silence was different when she was alone.

Beyond the circle of light, the furniture, boxes, and trunks loomed large. A sound, like the scurrying of a mouse, made Amy catch her breath. It came from the doll's house corner. Ellen and Aunt Clare seemed very far away.

Just close up the house and go downstairs, silly, she scolded. But she had to force herself to walk across the attic. The sound came again—a small, frightening scratch.

Biting her lip, Amy stepped into the shadows around the doll's house. In spite of the lingering warmth of the day, the corner seemed cold. She dropped to her knees in front of the house and swung the façade shut. For a moment, before the wall clicked into place, she stared into the dim rooms. Then she was on her feet and running back across the attic and down the stairs.

"Amy! Your aunt's calling us—" Ellen was in the hall at the bottom of the stairs. She stepped back, startled, as Amy burst out. "Hey, what's the matter with you?"

"Nothing," Amy said. "Nothing's the matter. It's just creepy up there when you're all alone. Come on, let's go downstairs."

She didn't want to think about the attic any more today. She didn't want to talk about the doll's house. If she did, she'd have to work out how one of the dolls—Grandma Treloar it was—could be standing in the sitting-room when Amy was practically certain they'd left the whole family sitting round the dining-room table.

Dolls can't move by themselves, she told herself, and felt goose pimples pop up on her arms.

6.

"A Visit You'll Remember"

"I should go home," Ellen said. "I told my mother I'd be back by seven." But she didn't move. They'd been sitting out on the front steps for nearly an hour. The biscuits-and-fudge snack had expanded to include sandwiches and milk, while the night closed in around them. For the last twenty minutes they'd been watching two rabbits—small, dark mounds with pointed ears—foraging for their supper in the deepening twilight.

"We'll drive you home when you're ready," Aunt Clare said. "No rush."

"It's so peaceful here." Ellen sounded dreamy. "I'd love to live in the country—even if it is sort of spooky."

Spooky. The image of the grandmother doll

standing in the doll's house sitting-room flashed through Amy's mind. What would Ellen say if she knew about that? Amy swept the image away.

"I like the country, too," she agreed. "Look! Did you see that bird swoop across the garden?"

"That bird was a bat," Aunt Clare said. She chuckled as both girls ducked their heads. "You're right, Ellen, it *is* peaceful. But there's a lot of work in a big old country house like this one. It's so full of *things*—and I've promised Amy's father that they'll all be gone before I go back to the city."

"Why don't you find a job in Claiborne?" Amy asked. "Then you could live here all the time." She pictured herself visiting Aunt Clare whenever she felt like it.

"I belong in Chicago," Aunt Clare said. Her voice was warm and relaxed, not at all the way it had sounded when she talked about the doll's house. "When I get this job done here—the house emptied and sold—I'll be ready to tackle Chicago again. At least, I hope so. But just now, I'm grateful to be here." She sounded as if she were thinking aloud.

Crash! A sound of falling metal shattered the night quiet. The two rabbits vanished into the bushes that edged the lawn. Amy felt a prickle of hairs at the back of her neck.

"Those damned raccoons." Aunt Clare jumped to her feet. "Now they aren't even waiting till we go to bed. Wait here, girls, I'm going inside to get a torch. Maybe we can scare *them* for a change."

She tiptoed across the porch and returned in a few moments with the biggest torch Amy had ever seen.

"Come on. And don't make a sound. Those rascals are probably so busy, they won't hear us coming if we're careful."

Smothering nervous giggles, Amy and Ellen fell in behind Aunt Clare, and they all tiptoed round the side of the house. The side garden was black except for patches of light outside the sitting-room windows.

"Stay close." Aunt Clare murmured. "I don't want to use the torch until we're nearer."

"What if it isn't a raccoon?" Ellen whispered. "What if it's a burglar trying to get into the house?"

Aunt Clare didn't answer. Ahead, there was a scuffling and a clanking of metal. Amy reached back and found Ellen's hand. "It's all right," she said.

"Now!" Aunt Clare switched on the torch. On the ground sat a large raccoon, its forelegs wrapped round a rubbish bin to hold it steady. A smaller raccoon was on top of the bin, tugging at the lid. Another bin lay on its side, the lid still on.

For a second the intruders stared, bright-eyed and terrified, through their dark furry masks. Then the bigger one scrambled up and raced into the darkness behind the garage. The bin tipped over, and the smaller partner somersaulted to the ground. With an outraged squeal, it ran off, too.

Aunt Clare laughed gleefully. "We gave them

a little of their own medicine!" she exclaimed. "Maybe they'll leave us alone for a few nights— though I doubt it." She swung the light back towards the girls and grinned at their expressions. "Well Ellen, how do you like country life now?"

"I still love it," Ellen replied at once. "I just can't stop shaking, that's all."

"Amy, how about you?"

"Mum would have called the police if she'd heard a noise in the dark like that. She'd never have gone out by herself. I wouldn't have, either—but it was fun!"

"Your mother and I react differently to a number of things," Aunt Clare said, leading the way back to the house. "When you've lived alone, you get used to solving your problems by yourself. You can't always wait for help."

Later, after they'd driven Ellen and her bike home in the car, Aunt Clare said, "I hope you don't think I was criticizing your mother, Amy," she said. "I know I'm blunt. The thing is, it never occurred to me to be afraid. Tonight I wanted you and Ellen to see the raccoons—if I'd thought it was a burglar, I wouldn't have let you come with me."

"I didn't think you were criticizing," Amy said. "I know Mum worries about things a lot. She can't help it." She remembered how daring she'd felt, walking through the darkness towards the unknown. "I really like solving problems myself. Being independent."

Still later, as Aunt Clare rinsed the supper plates and wiped the vinyl tablecloth, she said,

"Your sister must learn to be independent, too. She has to become her own person."

"Oh, no." Amy was shocked. "Louise's like a little kid. She'll always be that way. The doctor said so."

"I know." Aunt Clare rinsed the dishcloth and draped it over a tap to dry. "But even little kids can learn to help themselves, and they're happier because of it." She turned and smiled at Amy. "I've enjoyed having you and Ellen here today," she said. "You've made me feel about twelve years old myself. And speaking of ripe old ages, don't you have a birthday coming up soon?"

"Next Friday. Ellen's is the week after."

Aunt Clare clapped her hands. "How about a party?" she asked. "A birthday party for both of you. You and Ellen can invite some friends."

Amy could hardly believe her ears. A double birthday party—exactly what she'd suggested to Ellen yesterday.

"We'll make the pizza ourselves. I'm the best pizza maker you'll ever meet." Aunt Clare gave Amy a quick hug. "I want this to be a visit you'll remember."

Curled up in her high, rather lumpy bed that night, Amy wondered if every day with Aunt Clare would be as exciting as this one. Yesterday she'd been miserable. Today she had all kinds of things to think about. Ellen's friendship. The birthday party. Aunt Clare herself—wise, brave, unpredictable. The doll's house.

Amy's eyes closed, and at once, in the darkness

behind her eyelids, the doll's house appeared, as vividly as if it were there in the bedroom. *It's waiting,* Amy thought hazily. But waiting for what? She sank into uneasy sleep.

7.

"They Were Murdered?"

Most of the time, Amy enjoyed her holiday from sister-sitting. No one begged her to play baby games. No one insisted on going along every time she went out. No one hung around listening, asking questions, interrupting when Ellen came over after school. No one turned the television on full blast and then wandered away, or complained if Amy curled up with a book for hours.

Planning the double birthday party was a special treat. "Ellen and I have invited four girls to the party," Amy reported to Aunt Clare at dinner on Tuesday evening. "There were a couple of others we wanted, but they're busy."

"Four is fine." Her aunt poured extra sauce on Amy's spaghetti and passed her a wicker basket filled with garlic bread. "I'll do the shopping on Thursday. I'll get Italian sausage and pepperoni and mozzarella cheese and mushrooms. . ."

"Terrific! I called Mum and told her about the party. I said it was just going to be a few kids from our class. She'll make a birthday cake." There was no use mentioning how coolly her mother had taken the news of the party. "I'll bake a cake after Louise goes to bed," was what she'd said. "Her feelings would be hurt if she knew."

Amy wound long strands of spaghetti around her fork. "It's really nice of you to have this party," she said. "Ellen thinks so, too."

"Nonsense." There were tired lines around Aunt Clare's eyes that vanished when she smiled. "You're doing me a favour," she said. "I told your father the truth when I said I needed company for a while."

"Did you ever want to get married and have kids?" Aunt Clare would have been a great mother.

Amy was sorry at once that she'd asked. The tired lines came back, and for a moment her aunt looked old. "Most women want that at some time in their lives," she said shortly. "I'm no different."

"But you decided to have an exciting career instead," Amy suggested.

"When Grandma and Grandpa Treloar were—when they died, I went to work," Aunt Clare said. "I didn't have much choice. If I'd met the right person, I might have married and had a family, and a career, too. But I didn't."

46

Amy decided to change the subject. "Did Grandma and Grandpa die in a car crash?"

But that, too, was the wrong question. "It's all in the past, Amy," Aunt Clare said. She stared at the remaining spaghetti on her plate as if she couldn't remember what it was. "Obviously your father hasn't talked to you about your grandparents, and, frankly, I don't want to. That whole episode is something I'd like to forget. If possible." She crumpled her napkin beside her plate. "Have you had enough to eat? I think I'll just wash the dishes and turn in early, if you don't mind. I've been cleaning and sorting all day—I'm exhausted."

Amy jumped up. "I'll wash the dishes," she offered. "You go to bed."

For the rest of the evening, while Amy washed the dishes, did her homework, and watched television, Aunt Clare's suddenly taut, unhappy face was there in front of her. Why should Aunt Clare refuse to talk about how Grandma and Grandpa Treloar died?

Amy decided to find out, one way or another.

"Ask your father and mother," Ellen said the next afternoon after school. "They'd know."

"Of course they would," Amy replied. She and Ellen were wheeling their bikes up the steep hill beyond the high school. "But they won't tell me. They've always changed the subject when I've mentioned Great-Grandma and Great-Grandpa. Something bad must have happened to them—I'm sure of it. You should have seen Aunt Clare's face when I asked her."

"Still, if you asked your father. . ."

Amy shook her head. "I'm going to play detective and find out for myself. I know the year they died—1952—and I'm going to go through the obituaries in the *Claiborne News* for that year and see what I can learn. If it was an unusual accident, maybe there'll be a news article about it, too. Want to help me look?"

Ellen made a face. "That'll take hours, Amy," she said. "Going through stacks of old newspapers. Reading about dead people. Ugh!"

Amy admitted she had a point. "Go with me to the library just this once," she suggested. "Just today. We'll look for one hour—and if we don't find anything, I'll look by myself some other time."

"Well, all right," Ellen gave in.

The girls left their bikes at the rack in front of the library and made their way through the reading room to the information desk. Amy explained that she wanted to look at the 1952 issues of the *Claiborne News*.

"The films, you mean." Miss Tatlock, the assistant librarian, acted as if the request were a routine one. "Have you used a viewer before?"

"No." Amy rolled her eyes at Ellen. What were they getting into? She'd expected to sit down with a stack of newspapers, and start paging through them.

"Come along, then, I'll show you. This way—the audiovisual materials are in the back room." She led the way around the reference area, and soon Amy was seated in front of a screen about the size of the television screen at home. Ellen sat beside her, with her chair pulled up as close as possible.

Miss Tatlock went to a filing cabinet and pulled out four small cardboard boxes. She opened one and took out a spool of film.

"Now," she said, "all of the January 1952 *Claiborne News* is on this spool. You thread it through the machine, like this. You move it ahead fast with this knob, or rewind it with this one. Use the knob at the side to move ahead one page at a time. What are you looking for, exactly?"

Amy gulped. "Obituaries."

Miss Tatlock gave her a puzzled look. "Well they're on the second-to-last page of the paper now, and I bet they were there thirty years ago, too," she said. "Let's find out." She turned the knob at the side of the viewer five times in quick succession, and whole pages of the paper slid by on the screen. "There," she said. "Just as I thought. Very little changes in the *News* except the headlines. Now, just look over the page, and keep turning till you find what you want. If you don't find it in the first four films—"she paused, but Amy kept her eyes on the screen—"just call me and I'll get the films for the rest of the year."

"Okay," Amy said. "Thanks a lot."

She waited until Miss Tatlock had gone back to her desk, then began turning the side knob furiously. Pages of the second of January edition flashed by until she came again to the small print of the obituaries. There were no Treloars mentioned.

"This isn't going to take long," Amy said. She skipped through January, removed the film, and re-threaded the machine. February and March went by in quick succession.

"Hey, turn back to that first page," Ellen said, halfway through April. "Look at that headline: 'Flash Flood Sweeps Away Birthday Celebration.' Let's read about that."

The story told of a flood that had covered the west side of Claiborne with two metres of water. It had come so suddenly that people were barely able to escape. Marilyn Thompson's guests at her tenth birthday party had had to run for their lives, and her gifts had been carried away or ruined before she had a chance to open the parcels.

"Poor girl," Ellen said. "I bet she feels—felt—terrible."

"She'd be forty years old now," Amy said. It was an amazing thought. . . as if they'd peeked into another world that no longer existed.

"Spooky," Ellen commented. "I'll go out and ask the librarian for the rest of 1952. You can keep on looking."

She started towards the reference area but stopped when Amy gasped.

"What is it? Did you find something?"

Amy nodded. With a trembling finger she pointed at the screen. "Another front-page story," she said thickly. "Oh, Ellen, look."

Ellen hurried back and leaned over Amy's shoulder, her eyes widening. " 'Prominent Couple Murdered in Their Home,' " she read aloud. " 'Five-year-old Grandson Found

Hidden and Asleep in Cupboard.' " She stopped reading and stared at Amy. "Were those your great-grandparents? They were *murdered?*"

"And that's my father," Amy said, her voice quivering. "No wonder he never talks about how they died. My very own father was the five-year-old boy who was in the cupboard while his grandparents were being killed."

8.

"I Don't Believe in Ghosts"

The story was terse and ugly. The Treloars' granddaughter Clare had discovered the body of Margaret Treloar in the sitting-room when she returned home after going to a film with friends. Police were called, and they found James Treloar, fatally shot, on his bed in the couple's upstairs bedroom. The Treloars' little grandson, Paul, was at first believed to have been kidnapped, but when the police searched the house, they found him curled up fast asleep in a small wood cupboard next to the fireplace in the sitting room. There were no suspects.

"How terrible for Aunt Clare!" Amy exclaimed. "Think what it would be like, Ellen, coming home and finding them like that. . . ."

Stunned, she turned to the next day's paper.

There were interviews with the police inspector, the cleaning woman who came in three days a week to help the Treloars, and the handyman who took care of the garden and some of the household jobs. The police inspector said the search for clues was continuing. The Treloars' house was under guard, and the grandchildren were staying with relatives while funeral arrangements were made.

The murders were still front-page news on the third day. " 'Victims' Granddaughter in Shock,' " Amy read. "Ellen, listen to this. 'Clare Treloar, 18, is under a doctor's care after being told last evening that her friend Thomas Keaton was killed in a one-car accident on the night of her grandparents' murder. Keaton, who moved to Claiborne a year ago, was identified by a friend. His car was travelling north at high speed when it left the road and hit a tree. The accident was discovered by passers-by early yesterday morning.' "

"That's terrible," Ellen breathed. "Her boyfriend and her grandparents killed in one night!"

Amy's eyes were wet. "And guess who keeps asking her silly questions about it. Me! Oh, Ellen!" She was remembering the conversation at the dinner table the night before. "I even asked her why she didn't get married and have children of her own. How could I do that?"

"You didn't know. It's really something, though. All these years she's been faithful to her lost love. She probably cries herself to sleep every night."

Amy tried to imagine Aunt Clare—so brisk and merry one minute, so touchy and remote the next—crying into her pillow.

"Maybe," she said. "At least, this explains why the dolls and the doll's house bother her so much. They bring back a lot of really terrible memories."

"Darn!" Ellen looked at her watch. "I have to go home right now. We have dinner early on Wednesdays because dad goes bowling. I hate to leave. Are you going to read any more?"

Amy nodded. "I want to find out if they caught the murderer," she said. "Maybe the police found some clues in the next couple of days." She walked with Ellen as far as the information desk and requested films of the May and June 1952 papers. "I'll call you tonight and tell you what I find out," she promised.

"Won't your aunt be wondering where you are?"

"She doesn't worry as long as I get home before dark. I can make it if I stay another fifteen minutes or so." Amy waved good-bye to her friend and then followed Miss Tatlock back to the audiovisual room.

"Can't you find what you're looking for?" Miss Tatlock gathered up the first four tapes. "I can give you the whole year if you wish."

Amy said no. If the rest of the story of her great-grandparents' murders wasn't in the May and June papers, she'd have to come back another day. Hurredly, she skimmed through the films, but except for several short articles regretting that the police had been unable to solve the case, there was no more information until the last week in June. There it was reported that Clare Treloar was moving to Chicago and her little brother, Paul, was going to live with cousins.

Going home through the quiet streets and out into the countryside, Amy thought about what it had been like for Aunt Clare. How lonely she must have been during those first months in Chicago! Amy felt a wave of homesickness for her own family. It was hard to believe she'd only been away from them for a few days.

When she reached the house, her aunt was in the kitchen, spooning a fragrant sauce over browned pieces of chicken. "I hope you're starving," she said cheerfully. "This is my favourite recipe, but it's too much trouble to make if I'm just cooking for myself."

"I could eat the whole potful," Amy said.

All through the delicious dinner, Aunt Clare chatted about her plans for the house. Today she'd arranged for an appraiser to come in and look over the furniture. When that was done, she would set a day for an auction.

"I'll put aside what I want, and your father and mother can take what they want, and we'll get rid of everything else at the sale. What a relief that'll be!" She grinned at Amy. "This probably seems pretty dull stuff to you, but I'm going to feel like a new woman when this house is sold. Meanwhile, I'm glad we're going to have a party before we say goodbye to the old place."

"I want to go home tomorrow after school and pick up some tapes and my tape deck," Amy said.

Aunt Clare bit her lip. "Oh-oh!" she exclaimed. "I was supposed to tell you to call Louise as soon as you got home. She called and wanted to talk to you."

"Was anything wrong?" Amy felt a familiar twinge of guilt.

"I don't think so." But Aunt Clare sounded doubtful. "It's hard to tell, isn't it? She always seems kind of—gruff."

"She doesn't mean to sound that way," Amy said. "It's just that when she has something on her mind, she doesn't think about anything else."

Aunt Clare smiled. "You're an understanding sister."

"No, I'm not," Amy said, turning red. Was Aunt Clare being sarcastic? "I'd better call right now," she mumbled and hurried down the hall to the phone.

Louise must have been waiting. Her deep "Hello" broke into the first ring, and she began reciting her news as soon as she was sure it was Amy at the other end of the line.

"I know how to weave," she said. "I made a potholder."

"That's terrific, Louise. Did you learn how at school?"

"Mrs. Peck taught me. She's really smart. She taught me and she taught Marisa."

Marisa was Mrs. Peck's granddaughter. She was a year older than Louise and a classmate at Stadler School for Exceptional Children. Marisa stayed with her grandmother after school until her mother came to pick her up.

"My potholder is prettier than Marisa's," Louise went on. "I'll make you one if you want me to."

"Great," Amy said. "You can make one for Aunt Clare, too."

Silence. "Just you," Louise said finally. "When are you coming home, Amy?"

"Well, I'm dropping in tomorrow afternoon for a few minutes," Amy said. "I have to pick up some tapes for the—some tapes I want. I'll see you then, all right? Tell Mum."

"All right." Louise liked carrying messages. "Goodbye." The receiver clicked.

I shouldn't have told her I was coming. Amy thought. *I could have picked up the tapes while she was at Mrs. Peck's. She'll just get upset again when I leave.* But she felt better for having talked to her sister. If Louise was having fun with Mrs. Peck and Marisa, Amy didn't need to feel so guilty about being away.

She decided to call Ellen before doing her homework. "I checked through all of May and June," she said in a low voice. "They didn't find out who did the murders."

Ellen whistled. "Not even a clue? Amy, maybe the killer is still here in Claiborne. Maybe it isn't such a great idea to be living way out there in that old house. He might come back and—"

"After thirty years?" Amy scoffed. "Why would he do that?"

"Still," Ellen insisted, "I wouldn't like staying in a house where people were murdered. Even thirty years ago. It could be haunted."

Amy had been trying not to think about that.

The sitting-room where her great-grandmother had died was only a few metres away. "I don't believe in ghosts," she said, more bravely than she felt. "And I suppose Aunt Clare doesn't either, or she'd never have come back here to live, even for a short time. Listen, Ellen, do you want to go back to the library with me next week and check the rest of the tapes for 1952? Maybe they caught the killer later. The last thing I found today was an article about Aunt Clare going to Chicago and my father being adopted by some cousins—" The floor creaked behind her, and she whirled round to discover Aunt Clare standing there, white-faced, holding a large cardboard carton.

"I have to go. See you tomorrow." Amy hung up the phone. "It was Ellen," she said, unable to meet her aunt's eyes. "I'll carry that stuff. Where do you want it?"

Aunt Clare turned away. "It's some pieces of the best china," she said. Her voice cold. "I'm going to put them up in the attic with the rest of the set, so the appraiser can tell how much there is." She shot a furious glance over her shoulder. "You must have a lot more telephoning to do. Everybody loves hearing about a gory murder."

Amy felt as if she'd been slapped. "I wasn't gossiping, Aunt Clare—not really. I just wanted to know what happened to Grandpa and Grandma—and I haven't told anyone but Ellen. She was with me when I found the stories in the papers—"

Aunt Clare started up the stairs.

"I'm sorry," Amy said. "I know I keep saying

and doing the wrong things. But I don't mean to upset you."

"Don't bother to apologise." Aunt Clare snapped. "You admit you're curious—don't expect me to like it. The past is dead, and it would help a lot if you'd leave it that way. You needn't go back to the library, either. The police didn't find out who killed them."

At the bottom of the attic stairs she stopped and waited for Amy to open the door. "I think I'd like to be alone for a while," she said and went on up the steps, puffing a little with the weight of the box.

Amy was close to tears. This time she'd made a real mess of things. *Why didn't I wait till tomorrow to talk to Ellen?* she mourned. *Now Aunt Clare is disgusted with me, and I don't blame her.*

The hall was dark, the house very still except for Aunt Clare's steps overhead. With dragging feet, Amy made her way down the hall, past the bedroom where her great-grandfather had been killed. She had just reached her own room and had her hand on the light switch when a strangled cry broke the silence.

"Aunt Clare!"

Amy raced back down the hall. "Aunt Clare! Are you all right?"

There was no answer. Amy ran up the attic steps. Her aunt was standing in the far corner of the attic, staring in horror at the doll's house. "How could you do it?" she cried. "How could you do such a cruel, ugly thing?"

"Do what?" Amy hurried to her aunt's side.

The doll's house was open, and the small box that had held the dolls was open, too. The girl doll was back in the box. The grandfather doll lay down across the bed in the master bedroom, and the grandmother stood where Amy had last seen her, in the sitting-room.

Aunt Clare bent, robotlike, and reached into the sitting-room, carefully avoiding the doll that balanced against the bookcase. With a fingernail she loosened a tiny latch in the wall and opened the wood cupboard door next to the fireplace. The boy doll lay inside, its head pillowed on a log the length of a pin.

She stood up. "This is unforgivable, Amy," she said in a voice of ice. "I suppose you have a right to know our miserable family history—I can try to make myself understand your need to find out. But to make a game of the deaths of your own great-grandparents! How could you?"

"I di-didn't!" Amy's mouth was dry with shock and fright. "I haven't been up here since Saturday when I showed the doll's house to Ellen. We put all the dolls around the dining-room table, and that's how we left them. . ." Should she tell about seeing the grandmother doll in the sitting-room only minutes later? Her head whirled. "I mean," she said, "I think—"

"Don't make it worse by lying," Aunt Clare said. "I just can't imagine how you could—"

"But I closed the front of the house on Saturday," Amy protested. "I know I did! And I didn't put the dolls where they are now."

Aunt Clare just looked at her. "I'd appreciate

it if you'd put all the dolls back in the box where you found them and leave them there," she said. "Permanently."

Amy felt numb. She'd never been called a liar before. Trembling, she knelt and collected the dolls. She laid them in a row and closed the box with care. Then she stood up and faced her aunt.

"I really didn't move the dolls, Aunt Clare," she said. "And I didn't try to find out what happened to Great-Grandma and Great-Grandpa Treloar just so I could gossip with Ellen about it. I wanted to know! You wouldn't talk about it, and I knew my parents wouldn't either. So I decided to find out for myself."

She paused. Aunt Clare was staring into the doll's house, almost as if she didn't hear.

"I didn't move the dolls," Amy repeated. She searched for a way to prove she was telling the truth. "I just found out about the murders after school today, Aunt Clare, and I haven't been up in the attic since. You know I haven't."

"I don't know anything," Aunt Clare said, and now she sounded more sad than angry. She closed the doll's house and replaced the sheet that had covered it the first time Amy saw it. "If you didn't move the dolls, who did?" she asked. "Tell me that."

Amy couldn't answer.

9.

"I've Never Been So Scared in My Life"

Amy's notebook and English textbook were in the kitchen where she'd dropped them when she came home. She grabbed them and went back upstairs to her bedroom. Aunt Clare went into the sitting-room to watch television on the little portable set she'd brought with her from Chicago. They didn't look at each other as they passed in the hall at the foot of the stairs.

The bedroom felt chilly and impersonal. Amy dropped her schoolbooks on the bed and wandered around, thinking about her cozy bedroom at home, the bureau and desk tops covered with pictures and crystal bottles, the walls bright with posters, snapshots, and pennants. The shelves of books and miniatures. The friendly clutter. There was nothing in this room to remind her of home except Louise's vase, standing on top of the bureau. Amy picked it up and ran a finger over the lacquered roses. She would have given anything to see Louise sitting at the foot of her bed right now.

I'm scared, she thought. *I've never been so scared in my life.* It was bad enough to be screamed at and accused of lying. Aunt Clare was the most up-and-down person Amy had ever known. But it was the doll's house, and the dolls that didn't stay where they were put, that really frightened her. What was happening in the attic? Who—or *what*—had moved the dolls?

She went to a window. The night was mild, sweet-smelling, and tinted with a pale wash of moonlight. *I can call Mum from school tomorrow and tell her I want to come home.* Her mother and Louise would be pleased. Her father would be disappointed. He really liked the idea that she and Aunt Clare had become friends.

Amy turned to the bed and kicked off her shoes. She sat cross-legged with the pillows piled behind her and opened her English book on her lap. But she couldn't concentrate. The words ran together when she tried to read.

Maybe the ghost—if there was a ghost—had a special reason for moving the dolls. If Amy went home, the reason would remain a secret. Aunt Clare would finish her work on the house and leave. She'd go on believing that Amy had lied about moving the dolls. If there were a ghost, it would be ignored.

No one knows there's a mystery here except me. Amy thought, shivering. *I have to stay, even if*

Aunt Clare hates me.

Downstairs the television murmured. A breeze lifted the curtains, and an owl hooted in the distance. Amy bent over her book and started to read again. The homework was a detective story. She wished it were something else, a funny essay would have been nice. She was jumpy enough without reading about another dark old house full of secrets.

An hour later she closed the book. She'd jotted down the answers to the questions at the end of the story, and in the morning she'd copy them out during her second-hour free lesson.

She undressed quickly. As she returned from the bathroom, the television clicked off downstairs. She heard Aunt Clare's light steps moving around the house as she turned out the lights. Amy closed the door of her room and jumped into bed, pulling the covers up to the tip of her nose. *Sleep*, she commanded herself. *Don't think. Sleep.*

But sleep wouldn't come. She listened to her aunt come upstairs, heard her go into her bedroom, to the bathroom, and back to her room again. What was she thinking now? Maybe she was deciding how to get rid of a no-longer-welcome guest.

The owl hooted again, closer this time. Amy felt herself drifting, half awake, half asleep. Strange thoughts fluttered through her head—scraps of dreams, bits of conversation. She saw Louise holding up a pot-holder that glittered with golden threads and sparkled with diamonds. She saw Mrs. Peck, her arm round

Louise's shoulders, motioning Amy to go away. She saw Aunt Clare standing in front of the doll's house, her mouth open in a silent cry.

Then she woke up.

The breeze had died down, and the curtains hung motionless. Amy raised her head and looked around the room. Someone was at her door. She stared, wide-eyed, as the old-fashioned metal knob turned ever so slowly in the moonlight.

Amy cowered under the covers. Her stomach churned. She squeezed her eyes shut, willing this to be another bad dream. But when she looked again, the knob was still turning. Something was out there in the hall, trying to get in.

A crash shredded the stillness. Amy screamed, a shrill wail that seemed to come right from her toes. The door flew open. Aunt Clare stood there, looking like a ghost in her long nightgown. Her face was as white as the gown.

"Aunt Clare! What's happening?"

Her aunt ran across the room to the window that overlooked the back yard. "It's those blasted raccoons again," she said. "Two of them are running across the lawn."

Amy sat bolt upright in bed, one fist pressed against her mouth. If she moved, she'd start screaming again.

"Amy, it's all right. Really! Just raccoons prowling for their dinner. I warned you that it might happen—"

"It—it's not j-just that—" Amy's teeth were actually chattering. "I saw the doorknob turn—"

"Oh, my." Aunt Clare came over to the bed. "I'm sorry, I wanted to peek in very quietly and see if you were asleep. I wanted to talk . . ."

Amy leaped out of bed. For this moment at least, talk was impossible. The doll's house, the angry scene in the attic, the moving door knob, and now the raccoons, were too much. "I can't—" she began, and gave up. She raced down the hall, to the bathroom, both hands over her lips, and got there just in time.

When she returned, the lamp on the bedside table was lit, and Aunt Clare was sitting in the rocker. Her feet were drawn up under her gown, and she looked almost like a little girl. She waited while Amy climbed back into bed and pulled up the covers.

"Better now?"

Amy considered. "A bit. But I'm cold. I can't stop shaking."

"Shall I close the windows?"

"No. I'll be all right in a couple of minutes." Amy remembered something her mother often said. "I have a nervous stomach."

"Well, it's had plenty to be nervous about this evening," Aunt Clare said. "I'm sorry I blew up at you, Amy. That's what I came to say—and scared you nearly to death in the process. I know I overreacted to that whole business up in the attic this evening."

Amy took a deep breath. Aunt Clare believed she was telling the truth, after all.

"That's all right," Amy said. "I just didn't want you to think I'd lie to you."

Her aunt leaned forward. "I don't want you to

think you *have* to lie to me," she said. "That's what's bad about all of this. We're friends—we should be able to be honest with each other."

Aunt Clare *didn't* believe her.

"It's been such a dreadfully long time since I was twelve years old," her aunt continued. "Kids are different now—you see so much violence on television and in the films, I can understand how you might be fascinated by. . . by what happened to your great-grandparents. It was just that seeing the dolls put into the rooms where Grandma and Grandpa were found that night brought back so much pain. . ." She sighed. "I really am sorry I made such a scene about it."

Amy opened her mouth to protest, then changed her mind. If she denied moving the dolls again, it would only make Aunt Clare angry once more. "I'm sorry, too," she said. "I know you want to forget all that."

"Yes, I do. And not just for the obvious reasons—the ones you read about in the newspapers. This was a very unhappy house, Amy—at the time Grandma and Grandpa were killed and for quite a while before. I was engaged to a man they didn't like at all. He was several years older than I was, very handsome, very headstrong. He drank quite a bit. Grandpa and Grandma didn't drink at all, and when he came to the house drunk one night, they ordered him out and said I was never to see him again. I was furious! We fought for months! I kept on seeing him secretly, then came home to their lectures. It was—awful." She had tears

67

in her eyes. "I told them I hated them," she said in a whisper. "They died thinking that was true."

Amy sat up. "Oh, but they didn't believe that," she said. "People say lots of things they don't mean. I do, when I'm angry with my mother. But she knows I'm sorry later. You can't still blame yourself, after all this time."

Aunt Clare stretched her legs and stood up. "Oh, yes, I can," she said softly. "You don't know how much." She patted Amy's arm. "You go to sleep now," she said. "I know I shouldn't burden you with all this, but after my outburst tonight, I think you have a right to know a *little* more about what happened. And why I'm the way I am—even after all these years." She smiled. "Shall we forgive and forget?"

"Of course." Amy lay back. "Thanks for telling me, Aunt Clare."

"Goodnight."

"Goodnight."

"The door closed, leaving Amy with the uncomfortable feeling that Aunt Clare had told only part of what was troubling her. What had really happened in this house so many years ago? Amy wondered if she'd ever know. And what strange things were happening here now?

This is a sad place, she thought, as she had before. The sadness was not just upstairs in the doll's house; it was all round her.

10.

"When She Leaves, Where Will I Run?"

It was nearly five when Amy cycled into the drive of her own house. She had never thought much about the house before—it was just the place where she lived—but now she knew that dark-grey clapboard and white shutters were the prettiest combination possible. Red and yellow tulips were in full bloom on either side of the front path, and the lilac bush next to the back door filled the air with its scent.

The garage was empty, which meant that her mother was not yet home from work. Amy used her key to let herself in, then wandered from room to room. She looked at her mother's crewel work on the walls and Louise's crayon drawings taped to the refrigerator. In front of her father's big armchair Amy stopped for a moment, then she sat down and pressed herself into the cushions. The chair smelled of pipe smoke, and there was a scattering of tobacco in the ashtray on the table. Amy picked up the tray and emptied it in the waste bin under the kitchen sink.

Upstairs in her bedroom, she laid her tape recorder on her bed and sorted through a stack of tapes to find the ones she wanted. There were other things she needed as well—the bath powder that had been a Christmas gift from Louise, the favourite T-shirt she planned to wear at the party. Dental floss. An extra ballpoint pen. As she was dropping her things into a shopping bag, a car door slammed.

Amy dashed downstairs and threw her arms round her mother. Then she hugged Louise. Louise's face was flushed and smiling.

"Look, Amy," she said and plunged a hand into a sack she carried. "I made a puppet today. Look, Amy, look!"

Louise fitted the sock puppet over her hand. She poked a finger up into the stuffing inside. The head bowed and nodded, and Louise laughed. "Like the puppets at the arcade." she cried. "Only nicer. Isn't he nicer, Amy?"

"Yes, he is," Amy agreed. "Did you make that at school?"

"Mrs. Peck showed us how. I love Mrs. Peck. We make things every day."

Amy and her mother exchanged glances. "Each afternoon they decide what they're going to do the next day," Mrs. Treloar said with a funny little grimace. "Louise can hardly wait to get there after school. Tomorrow they're going to take a bus to the mall together—Mrs. Peck and Louise and Marisa. Mrs. Peck thinks the girls should learn how to take the bus by themselves."

"But they can't!" Amy exclaimed. "They'll get lost, Mum."

"Will not!" Louise thrust the puppet into Amy's face. "Will not!" she roared. "I can do it!"

"Calm down," Mrs Treloar ordered. "We'll talk to your father about it tonight. Mrs. Peck has Marisa doing a lot of things Louise doesn't do. She goes to the grocer's all by herself, and she has a little garden, and—"

"Marisa is older," Amy said. She pushed away the stocking puppet impatiently. "Marisa is—" She was going to say "cleverer," but the look on Louise's face stopped her in time. Besides, she didn't really know Marisa, except for a glimpse or two when the girls got off their school bus. "Marisa is different," she finished lamely.

"Not!" Louise shrieked. "We're just the same."

Amy shrugged. She couldn't work out why the thought of Mrs. Peck teaching Louise to do things was so irritating. But it was. Clearly, Mrs. Treloar wasn't especially pleased either.

Louise is ours, Amy thought. *That's it. We know what she can do and what she can't do. We don't need any Mrs. Peck trying to change things.*

But that was a silly way to feel. They did need Mrs. Peck—at least, Amy did, if she was going to enjoy the visit with Aunt Clare.

71

"Well, it's up to you and Dad, I suppose," Amy told her mother in a low voice, while Louise sniffed and rubbed her eyes. "I'd better go—I told Aunt Clare I'd be back early because we have some things to do tonight to get ready for the party—" Damn! The word had slipped out before she could stop it. Amy almost groaned out loud. This was certainly her day for saying the wrong thing.

"Party?" The puppet dangled, forgotten, from Louise's hand. "What party? I want to go, too. Mum!"

Mrs. Treloar shook her head. "Amy's having a few friends over at Aunt Clare's tomorrow night—nothing special. We'll have her *real* birthday party right here when she comes home again. We'll have a cake and we'll play games, and you can invite Marisa—"

But Louise was not to be sidetracked. "I want to go to the party at Aunt Clare's house," she cried. "I want to go to *that* party."

"Well, you can't." The words were sharper than Amy had intended. She was disgusted with herself, and she was angry at her mother, too. *Why does she always make me feel like a selfish monster? Why can't she—just once!—say "This is Amy's birthday party, and she and her friends have a right to be alone"?*

That would never happen. With a despairing look at Louise's tear-streaked face, Amy ran upstairs to her bedroom. The shopping bag lay at the foot of the bed; she grabbed it and raced back downstairs.

"I have to go," she said. She felt strange and

stiff, as if she were talking to strangers instead of to her own family. "Say hi to Dad for me."

Her mother followed her to the front door, edging round Louise. "I'll have your birthday cake ready tomorrow afternoon," she said coolly. "Your father can drop it off on his way to Madison. He has a weekend seminar, and he wants to be there tomorrow night. The meetings begin early Saturday morning."

"Thanks, Mum." Amy didn't meet her mother's eyes. "I'm sorry..." They both looked at Louise, who had turned her back to them and was leaning against the wall.

"I suppose you are," Mrs. Treloar said with a sigh. "It seems like such a little thing—including your sister in your birthday party—but it's up to you. I suppose I can take her out for a hamburger or something when I get home from work."

Amy fled to her bike. She fairly flew down the drive, steadying the shopping bag that was crammed into the bike basket, and swung out on to the street. Houses streaked by, blurred by her tears.

Right now, she had Aunt Clare to go to. But Aunt Clare didn't want to stay in Claiborne; she could hardly wait to get back to the city.

What'll I do then? Amy wondered. *When she leaves, where will I run to?*

11.

"I Saw a Light in the Doll's house"

The smell of hot caramel met Amy when she opened the back door. Aunt Clare was at the kitchen table, gently stirring a huge batch of popcorn to coat it with syrup.

"Soup and salad for supper tonight," she announced when she saw Amy. "We have more important things to do than cook dinner."

Amy helped herself to a handful of caramel popcorn. It was good to see a smile after the painful scene at home.

"This tastes marvellous. Ellen will go crazy—caramel corn is her favourite thing in the whole world. What else are we going to have?"

"Fudge," Aunt Clare said. "Tons of fudge. That's *my* favourite. Not that I'm going to hang around the party and make a pest of myself—I do remember what it's like to have adults watching every move you make. But we'll cook a double batch, and then tomorrow night I'll go off to my room after you've eaten, and I'll take along a whole plateful, just for me. And how about egg rolls? I have the most marvellous recipe for egg rolls—"

"With pizza?" Amy giggled. Her aunt's enthusiasm was irresistible.

"You're right. A terrible idea! But I bought a huge bag of potato crisps on the way home, and the makings for a very special dip. How does that sound?"

"Terrific!" Amy was feeling better by the minute. "I'll run upstairs with the stuff I brought from home—oh, Mum said Dad will drop off the cake tomorrow afternoon. He's going out of town, and he'll bring it on the way."

"That'll be fine," Aunt Clare covered the bowl of popcorn with foil and set it at the end of the table. "How did it go at home?" she asked. "Everything back to normal?"

Amy didn't want to talk about home. "It was all right," she said. "I wasn't there very long."

"How's Louise getting along with the sitter?"

"All right, I suppose. They make things." Amy changed the subject. "Shall I get out the sugar and butter for the fudge?"

Aunt Clare nodded. "It's perfectly obvious Louise needs other people in her life. It isn't fair to expect her family to carry the whole burden. I know I've offended your mother by saying that, but I couldn't help speaking up the first night I had dinner at your house."

So that was it. That was why Amy's mother turned cool and quiet every time Aunt Clare was mentioned.

"Anyway," Aunt Clare continued, "we have work to do at the moment, right? Do we have enough chocolate for a double batch of fudge? Let me check. And you can open a tin of soup—whatever you like."

By the time they had eaten, set the fudge to cool, and mixed up the dip—which turned out to have fourteen ingredients—it was after nine.

"There's one more thing we ought to do this evening," Aunt Clare said. "You mentioned you'd like Ellen to stay overnight, didn't you?" Amy nodded. "Then we must get out an extra blanket and air it. There's a chest in the attic packed full of blankets and quilts. They're in good condition, even after all this time—but definitely musty. You run up and pick out one for Ellen. I'll hang it on the clothes line to air tomorrow, before I start cleaning."

Amy's stomach did a sharp flip-flop. She wasn't ready to go up to the attic. Not for a while.

"The nights aren't very cool now," she protested. "Ellen might not even want a blanket."

"Of course she'll want one," Aunt Clare said. "At least, there should be one in her room if she needs it."

"But I'm not sure I can find the chest."

"It's just at the top of the stairs on the left. A big metal box. You can't miss it." Aunt Clare gave Amy a look, and Amy knew she was sending a message. *She wants me to know she trusts me to go up there without moving the dolls.*

There was no way out. She'd have to get the blanket. Amy left the kitchen and went down the dimly lit hall to the stairs. *I wont't even look at the doll's house corner,* she promised herself. *I'll grab the top blanket and run.*

At the attic door, she hesitated. Maybe she could give Ellen her own blanket instead of getting another one. No, Aunt Clare would surely ask questions.

"Amy!" It was Aunt Clare calling from the kitchen. "I forgot to tell you, I think the light has gone in the attic. Take the big torch that's on the table next to my bed."

Oh, great! Amy's heart thudded as she switched on a lamp in Aunt Clare's room and searched for the torch.

She was halfway up the stairs, the torch beam bobbing on the steps in front of her, when she heard a small sound. *Mice. Please let it be mice.* A funny thing to wish, considering how much she hated mice. She stood still. The sound stopped, too, for just a moment, then began again. Something was moving around in the darkness above her.

The trunk on the left at the top of the stairs. Amy said the words to herself, trying to close out every other thought. When she reached the top step, she saw the big metal chest right where Aunt Clare had said it would be. She leaned over to loosen the fastenings with trembling fingers. *The top blanket,* she told herself. *Quick!*

The rustling, scraping sound grew louder. It

was coming from the doll's house corner. Without really meaning to, Amy swung the torch beam across the attic. The sheet that had covered the house was on the floor in a white heap. The house gaped open.

Amy's knees turned to jelly. The torch slipped from her fingers. When she tried to bend down and pick it up, she couldn't move. All she could do was stare at the house, and at the eerie glow that was beginning to fill the doll's house sitting-room.

A light in the doll's house. Amy squeaked in terror and dropped to a crouch. Her fingers closed on the torch, and she clattered down the steps, stumbling on the last one and hurtling into the hall. With a sob she slammed the door behind her and leaned against the wall.

"Amy! What on earth are you doing up there?" It was Aunt Clare again. "Did you find a blanket?"

"Everything's all right," Amy quavered. Her voice sounded as if it belonged to someone else. "I dropped the torch, but it didn't break." She paused, willing her aunt to stay downstairs. "I suppose I'll do my homework now and go to bed. I'm tired."

"That's fine. Pleasant dreams."

What a joke that was! As Amy pulled off her clothes and fumbled with the buttons of her pyjamas, she was more wide-awake and more frightened than she'd ever been in her life. After a moment's thought, she pushed the rocking chair across the room and hooked its back under the door so that no one—and nothing—could open it without her knowing. Then she climbed into bed and pulled the sheet over her head.

I saw a light in the doll's house. The words rattled around in her brain. And she'd seen even worse. In the second before she ran down the stairs, something had moved in the doll's house sitting-room. Something small and standing on two feet.

Not a mouse, Amy whimpered under the sheet. *Oh, I wish it had been a mouse!*

12.

"I've Come for the Party"

"Happy birthday, dear Amy!" Aunt Clare started to sing as Amy came into the kitchen, then stopped short. "You look terrible. Don't tell me you're coming down with something. Not on the day of your party!"

"I'm fine." Amy tried to sound as if she didn't have a thing on her mind except being a year older. "I just didn't sleep very well."

"I should think not." Aunt Clare put a hand on Amy's forehead. "You're not feverish, but what circles under those eyes! Why couldn't you sleep, for heaven's sake?"

Amy sat down and busied herself with cereal, sliced bananas, and milk. "I suppose I was just excited about the party," she lied. "It's really nice of you to do all this for Ellen and me, Aunt Clare."

"You know I love it," Aunt Clare said. "It's great to have a daughter even if it's just for a short time. And it'll be nice having Ellen to stay overnight, as well. Did you find a blanket for her?"

Amy gulped. "I'll get it as soon as I'm through eating," she promised. "It was so . . . so dark up there last night, I decided to wait until morning to get one."

"Well, never mind, I'll do it." Aunt Clare poured coffee into a big, old-fashioned mug and lifted it to her lips. "I was just feeling lazy by the time we finished making the fudge last night. Today I'm bursting with energy."

Amy shook her head quickly. "No, I'll do it. I want to." Aunt Clare mustn't go upstairs, she'd find the house uncovered and open and be certain Amy had done it.

I should have called her to the attic to see what I saw last night. Amy thought for the hundredth time. But she had been too frightened then to think clearly. All she'd wanted was to get out of the attic as fast as possible.

As soon as breakfast was over, Amy went upstairs and collected her schoolbooks from her room. She laid the books and her notebook in a neat pile at the top of the stairs, and then, taking a deep breath, she marched to the attic door and opened it.

Sunlight streamed through the dusty windows above her. She climbed the stairs slowly, wishing with every step that she didn't have to go through with this—wishing she were a thousand kilometres away. When she reached the top, she opened the metal chest quickly and took out a neatly folded blue blanket.

"Amy?" It was Aunt Clare calling from the lower hall. "Shall I come and help you? Is the catch on the chest hard to open?"

"No!" Amy shouted. "You don't need to come. I'll be down in a minute." *As soon as I do one other thing.*

She had to close the doll's house. No matter how frightened she was, she couldn't take a chance on Aunt Clare's finding the house open.

She slipped out of her shoes and tiptoed across the floor to the doll's house corner. The sheet still lay in a heap. The box that had held the dolls was open. Only the girl doll was inside.

Amy forced herself to look into the house. The grandfather doll was upstairs in the bedroom again, lying across the bed the way she and Aunt Clare had found him two nights ago. The grandmother was back in the sitting-room, facing the bookshelves that were built across one wall.

Amy's stomach turned over and she wondered if she were going to be sick. The grandmother doll, in its blue silk dress, had been moving in the sitting-room the night before, or it had been moved by hand no one could see.

Try to make Aunt Clare believe that!

Shakily, Amy reached round the grandmother doll and loosened the latch on the wood cupboard next to the fireplace. The tiny door opened, revealing the boy doll inside. Amy jumped back as if she'd been stung. With a sweep of her hand she slammed shut the front of the house, hiding the dolls from view. Then she scooped up the sheet and dropped it over the roof. With the toe of her trainer she flipped the cover of the doll box and pushed the box back out of sight.

"Amy? What are you doing up there? There's a phone call for you."

"Coming." Amy ran back to where she'd left her shoes and the blanket. Aunt Clare was waiting in the second-floor hall.

"You must have looked over every blanket in that chest," she teased. "Do you really think Ellen is going to care what colour you give her?"

Amy's knees were still shaking, but it was such a relief to get out of the attic—to have the dreaded errand over—that she felt giddy.

"Ellen won't care about anything as long as we give her lots of caramel corn!" she explained. She thrust the blanket into Aunt Clare's arms, snatched up her school books and ran downstairs to the telephone.

It was her mother, still sounding a little cool but determined not to spoil the birthday. "Have a lovely day, Amy. Your cake is all ready, and I must say it looks beautiful."

"Thanks, Mum."

"Louise wants to say happy birthday, too. She's right here."

"Happy birthday, Amy." Louise sounded depressed. Amy could imagine their mother standing next to the phone, wanting things to be right between her daughters.

"I'll see you in a couple of days, for sure," Amy promised. "We'll have a party, just the way

Mum said. All right?"

"All right."

When she hung up, Aunt Clare was in the hall, watching her. "I don't see why you have to feel apologetic about this party tonight," she said. "I'm sure your mother doesn't want that."

Amy shrugged. She knew what her mother wanted.

"Cheer up now. Today you're a teenager, and they're supposed to have plenty of problems without borrowing extra ones."

"Right," Amy said. "I have to find a boyfriend."

"And think about a career."

"And wear eye make-up."

"And learn all the new dances."

"And get to school on time!" She ran downstairs.

"See you tonight, Aunt Clare."

Today I'm a teenager. Amy said the words to herself as she cycled to school. Growing up meant taking responsibilities, and she was doing that. She was protecting Aunt Clare from the painful memories and guilt feelings that upset her so much. And protecting Aunt Clare meant not telling what she'd seen in the attic last night. She couldn't even tell Ellen without feeling like a traitor.

She stopped at an intersection while two small girls darted in front of her. They giggled as they ran.

I used to be like that, Amy thought, *when I was a little kid.* Suddenly it seemed a long time ago.

The school day dragged by. Ellen was full of plans for the party. Her mother would deliver all the guests to Aunt Clare's house at six, and another parent would pick them up—except Ellen, of course—at eleven. Cissie Talbott had a fortune-telling game she wanted to bring, and Kathy Sells had talked her cosmetician-aunt into giving her a box full of make-up samples. They could practise making themselves gorgeous. After the pizza. "Fat and gorgeous." Ellen sighed. "Oh, well."

"Aunt Clare made caramel popcorn," Amy said wickedly. "But if you think it's too fattening—"

Ellen groaned. "I'll blow up and burst, but I'll die happy," she said. "Oh, I wish it were six o'clock right now."

Amy wished it, too. But when the bell finally rang ending her last class for the day, she was glad there were a couple of hours left for the final preparations. The pizza should be all ready to pop into the oven when the girls arrived. Amy had never made pizza, but she intended to watch Aunt Clare carefully and learn. Next time, she'd be able to do it all herself.

She rode her bike home from school, hoping her father would be at Aunt Clare's with the cake when she turned into the garden. She missed him—perhaps because he always seemed like an island of calm in the midst of the storms that marked her relationship with her mother.

Aunt Clare came out on the back porch and stood there while Amy wheeled her bike into the garage.

"Did Dad bring the cake?"

Her aunt nodded. "About an hour ago. He was very sorry to miss you." She came down the steps, an odd expression on her face.

"What's the matter?" Amy demanded. "He's all right, isn't he?"

"He's fine," Aunt Clare said. "Nothing's wrong—I mean, not really. I just know you're going to be upset, and I'm sorry about it. I don't want anything to spoil this evening for you."

"What is it?" Amy followed Aunt Clare's glance and ran up the steps to the back door. "Something *is* wrong, I can tell—"

She burst into the kitchen and skidded to a stop. Louise was sitting at the table eating biscuits and drinking milk.

"Hello, Amy." She smiled brightly, through a milky moustache. "I've come for the party."

Amy felt Aunt Clare's hand on her shoulder. "It was an emergency," she said. "Do you remember you mother's friend Barbara? She lives in Sun Prairie, just outside Madison. She called around midday and asked if your mother could come and help her for a day or two. Her husband must have an operation—very unexpected—and there are two small children. . ." She stopped for breath. "Your mother felt she couldn't say no, particularly since your father was driving out that way this afternoon. They tried to get Mrs. Peck to take Louise for the weekend, but she's going with her granddaughter and the family to a cottage for a couple of days. There was just no other way—"

"Mum could have taken Louise with her," Amy said. "She could have done that if she'd wanted to."

Aunt Clare didn't argue. "I know how you feel—"

"No, you don't."

"I've come to the party," Louise repeated, but timidly now. She was watching Amy's expression. "Mum said I could. Dad and I brought the birthday cake. Look at it, Amy." She pointed to a big box on the table.

Amy went over to the box. The cake was pale yellow, with roses in clusters around the delicate green script. *Happy Birthday, Amy and Ellen.* There was a big *13* below the words.

"It's a beautiful cake," Aunt Clare said. "Your mother must have worked on it for hours."

Amy's eyes blurred with tears. She hated the cake. It was a bribe to make Amy let Louise come to her party.

"I bet there's nothing wrong with Barbara's husband," she said. "I bet he'd be surprised if he found out he's supposed to be in the hospital."

"Oh, Amy!" Aunt Clare sounded shocked. "You don't really believe that."

"Yes, I do. My Mother doesn't care what I want—ever!"

Louise's face crumpled. "I want to go home," she whimpered. "I don't like it here. You're horrid, Amy!"

"Girls!" Aunt Clare looked helplessly from one to the other. "It's going to be all right." She tried to put her arm round Amy's shoulders, but Amy pulled away. Then she went to Louise, circling her warily, as if she were from another planet. "If we can all just calm down for a minute," she pleaded. "Let's talk this over like grown-ups. . ."

Amy ran out of the kitchen and up the stairs to her bedroom. She didn't want to calm down. She didn't want to grow up and be reasonable and take responsibility—not if it meant taking care of Louise every day of her life. She was shaking with anger, and with something else—a feeling too dark to cope with in front of anyone else. For she had suddenly realised it wasn't just the birthday cake she hated. At the moment, she hated her mother, too.

13.

"Something Little Will Turn Out to be Big"

When Amy came back downstairs, Louise was watching Aunt Clare roll pizza dough on the kitchen table. A bowl of tomato sauce stood at one end of the table next to another of cheese, and the spicy smell of freshly browned sausage filled the room.

"Hello." Aunt Clare lunged at the circle of dough with the rolling pin, as if attacking it made her feel better. "You all right?"

"Yes." Amy met her aunt's eyes. "I'm sorry, I just don't like being tricked—"

"Well, I'm sure you're wrong about that," Aunt Clare interrupted smoothly. She folded the circles of pastry into quarters for easy handling and transferred them to greased baking sheets. "Here, party girl, it's your turn to work on the refreshments. Louise has broken up the cheese into small pieces, and the sausage is all ready. Just sprinkle plenty of each over the crusts, while I mince some garlic for the tomato sauce. This is an old family recipe—straight out of *Better Homes and Gardens*."

Amy brought the frying pan from the stove and set to work. She felt exhausted, and she knew her eyes were red from the storm of tears that had filled the last half-hour.

"I helped Aunt Clare," Louise said. She pushed the bowl of cheese across the table, watching Amy uneasily. "I did the cheese."

"Good for you." Amy knew she sounded cranky. "You did a good job," she added. "These are going to be great pizzas."

The uneasiness vanished at once. "These are going to be great pizzas," Louise agreed. "I'm going to tell everybody at the party that I helped."

Amy sighed. Her sister usually talked constantly when she had an audience, and because Amy's friends were unsure of how to react, they would pretend to be interested when they weren't. Amy could imagine just how the evening would go.

"I wish you'd try not to—" she began, then gave up. What was the use? The party was spoiled anyway. She wondered what Ellen would say—Ellen, who had called off their hike when she thought Louise would be coming along.

Aunt Clare seemed to guess her thoughts. "One thing to remember at the party, Louise," she said crisply, "is that all the girls will have things to talk about. I'm sure what they say will be interesting, so most of the time you must be a good listener."

Louise looked astonished. "I can't talk?"

"Of course you can talk. I said *most of the time*. Will you remember that?"

"Of course," Louise said. "I can listen. I can make puppets, too. I brought my puppet, Amy. I can show it to the girls at the party."

Amy cast a despairing look at her aunt. Louise was already thinking of it as *her* party. By the time the guests arrived, she'd be so excited there would be no calming her.

"Where will I sleep tonight?" Louise demanded. "I want to see."

Aunt Clare came back to the table with a saucer containing tiny slivers of garlic. "I suppose we can open up another bedroom," she said. "Louise can just ignore the dust. And we'll have to get some more bedding from the attic."

Amy shuddered. The last thing she wanted right now was another trip to the attic. "She can sleep with me," she said quickly. "She should, anyway. If she's in a room by herself, she might wake up in the middle of the night and come looking for me. She could get all mixed up in a strange house."

"Won't get mixed up," Louise protested. But she looked pleased with the answer to her question. "Show me where we sleep, Amy."

"You can go up and look at it," Amy replied. "It's the first room at the top of the stairs. Take your bag with you." She pointed at the duffel bag that stood next to the kitchen door.

When Louise had left, Amy picked up the bowl of tomato sauce. "I've finished with the cheese and sausage," she said. "Shall I spoon the sauce over the top?"

"Right," Aunt Clare replied. "I've put a tablecloth on the dining room table, with some small plates and glasses for Coke or whatever. I'll turn the oven on as soon as the girls get here."

"I'm really sorry about the way I acted—before," Amy mumbled. "I know it's not your fault the way things turned out."

"No, it isn't." Aunt Clare went to a window and looked out into the twilight. "You know, Amy, I feel sorry for Louise tonight. She knows very well she wasn't invited to your party, and she's uncomfortable, even if she doesn't show it much. She's accustomed to being smothered with attention. While you were upstairs, she kept saying she wanted to go home. I told her everything would be all right, but—"

"It will be," Amy said. "Don't worry. It was just seeing her here when I wasn't expecting her—"

"I know."

A car door slammed. "They're here." Amy said, grateful for the interruption. She hurried down the hall to the front door.

Ellen and Cissie were climbing out of the front seat of the Kramers' car. Three more girls spilled out of the back, giggling and bumping into each other as they sorted themselves out. Mrs. Kramer waved as Amy came down the front steps, and the car moved off down the driveway. "Happy birthday!" the girls shouted in a chorus.

The party had begun.

Since she fully expected to be miserable all evening, it took Amy a while to realize that everyone else was having a good time. The girls quickly settled on the sitting-room floor with soft drinks close by and the potato crisps and very special dip in the centre of the circle. Aunt Clare came in, briefly, to meet everyone, and Louise sat, cross-legged, next to Amy.

"My mother had to go away," Amy explained to Ellen in a low voice. And then to the others, "I guess you all know my sister Louise." Louise looked at them, speechless for the moment.

"This is great!" Kathy Sells exclaimed. "Friday night and a party, and next week school is over." She plunged a crisp into the creamy dip and leaned back. "I love this big old house, Amy. Lucky you, to be able to stay here. It's like a film set."

"A film set for a ghost picture," Midge Anders added. "If I lived here, I'd be looking for spooks around every corner."

If she only knew, Amy thought. "Is someone going to tell fortunes?" she asked, to change the subject.

"I am." Cissie produced a pack of cards from her bulging shoulder bag. "And Kathy has her aunt's make-up samples. She's going to show us how—"

"Your eyebrows look funny," Louise said to

93

Kathy, her shyness vanishing abruptly. "You look like you have crayon on them."

There was an embarrassed silence, and Amy felt her face grow hot. But Kathy just grinned. "I know I haven't got it right," she admitted. "Give me time, Louise. My aunt keeps saying 'Don't use too much,' but how do I know what too much is?"

They all laughed, and Amy relaxed. Louise crawled across the carpet to sit beside Kathy. "You're pretty anyway," she said. "You're nice."

Kathy looked pleased. "Well, thanks," she said. "I like your trouser suit, Louise. It's my favourite shade of blue."

Louise nodded. "It's nice," she agreed. "I picked it out with my Mum. Do you want to see the puppet I made?"

"What they want is food—in just a few minutes," Aunt Clare said from the hall. "How about helping me, Louise? You and I have important work to do."

Louise looked around regretfully but did as she was asked.

"Who wants to be first to have her fortune told?" Cissie spread out the cards and, without waiting for an answer, pointed at Ellen. "Birthday girls first," she said. "come over here and sit in front of the Great Zorina Who Tells All."

The cards showed that Ellen had a year of great happiness ahead of her. A blond man would come into her life. ("Probably the paper boy," Ellen groaned.) She would make a special new friend. ("That's you, Amy!") And she would be successful at whatever she did in the next two months. ("What I'm going to do for the next two months is sleep late every morning. I'll be a very successful sleeper.")

Amy had just taken Ellen's place in front of the Great Zorina when Louise returned. "The pizza's ready," she said. "I put it on the table, Amy."

The girls scrambled to their feet. "Pizza," Carol Thomas squealed, "that's all I want in my future."

Louise led the way into the dining room. "You sit here, Kathy," she ordered. "I'm going to sit next to you."

"You'd better sit next to me, Louise," Amy began, but Kathy took Louise's hand.

"You and I are friends, Louise," she said. "After supper I'll make you up like a film star.

"No eyebrows," Louise said, and looked surprised when everyone laughed.

For the rest of the evening, Louise hardly left Kathy's side. *Kathy's really wonderful*, Amy thought. *She treats Louise like a friend, not a pest. Why can't I do that?* But, of course, she reminded herself, Kathy didn't have Louise with her every day. It was easy enough to be patient for a couple of hours.

Aunt Clare stayed out of sight while they ate, except for a time or two when Louise's voice drowned out all other conversation. Then she appeared at the door to the kitchen, looked at Louise hard, and gave a tiny shake of her head. Each time, Louise quietened down. She seemed to accept the reproof, as long as it was given discreetly.

When the pizza plates were empty, the girls carried them to the kitchen. Amy put a tape on her player, and Kathy set out the make-up samples after covering the table with newspaper. Each guest took a turn in front of the mirror—and cold-creamed away most of the results—and then Cissie produced her fortune-telling cards again.

"Come on, Amy, you're next. Don't you want to find out what's going to happen to you, now that you're thirteen?"

"I'm not sure," Amy replied, and meant it. So many strange things had happened recently, she wasn't sure she was ready to hear more.

The Great Zorina said the man in Amy's life was going to be tall and dark. "And you're going to make an important discovery. Something that seems little will turn out to be big."

"She's going to find a diamond ring," Midge guessed.

"Or an oyster with a huge pearl inside it," suggested Carol.

"The doll's house!" Ellen sang out. "It's the doll's house in the attic, Amy! Cissie said, 'Something little will turn out to be big'." She turned to the others, her eyes shining. "Oh, you have to see it. It's a perfect miniature of this house we're in right now. It's probably worth thousands of dollars."

"We can't go up there!" Amy snapped out the words, and the girls looked at her in surprise. "Aunt Clare doesn't want anybody touching it," she explained. "It's—like Ellen said, it's very valuable."

"Oh, Amy, we won't touch it," Ellen coaxed. "We don't even have to open it. If you say so, we'll just look at the outside and peek in the windows."

"What doll's house?" Louise demanded. "Where's the doll's house? I want to see the doll's house, Amy."

Amy's heart sank. Damn Ellen, anyhow. She should have told her not to mention the doll's house at the party. Now it was too late. Even if the other girls didn't insist, Louise would keep on begging.

"We can't—" she said weakly.

"Can't what?" Aunt Clare was back, with a bowl of caramel popcorn in either hand. "Here's something to fill up any remaining empty spaces—until it's time for the cake." The girls groaned. "What can't you do, Amy?"

"Show them the doll's house. Ellen told them—"

"I told them how really beautiful it is, Miss Treloar," Ellen interrupted, helping herself to a handful of caramel popcorn. "You wouldn't mind if we took just a quick look at it, would you? Please!"

Aunt Clare's lips tightened. She glanced at Louise, who was on her feet and peering into corners of the dining-room as if the doll's house might be hidden there. "Well," she said reluctantly, "I suppose if you really want to . . ."

"We do!" Cissie exclaimed. "Oh, we do!"

"Go ahead, then. You take them up to the

attic, Amy. I replaced the light bulb this afternoon. *Please,* don't touch anything in the house."

"We won't," Ellen cried. "Come on, everybody. Wait'll you see it!"

With dragging feet, Amy followed her friends up the stairs. Ellen was in the lead, with Louise right behind her, pink with excitement. When they reached the far corner of the attic, Ellen stepped back and pulled Amy to the front.

"You'd better take off the sheet, Amy," she said. "Your aunt will feel better if nobody else touches it."

Amy was stiff with dread. She didn't want to uncover the house. The thought of what she might see—another change that couldn't be explained—was terrifying. It took all her willpower to pick up the end of the sheet and pull it off the house. She hardly heard the gasps of delight as her friends gathered around.

"Peek in through the windows," Ellen urged. "Amy and I put all the dolls at the dining-room table, and they look just like real people sitting there. Oh, Amy." She knelt at Amy's feet. "Open the front and give everybody one little look. Your aunt won't mind—what harm can it do, anyway?"

'I don't think I'd better."

"I want to see," Louise begged. "Please, Amy, please, please, please. I want to see inside."

Amy released the latch that held the front of the house in place, and the wall swung back. The girls crowded closer and bent down. At first they were speechless; then they all talked at once.

"The grandfather clock!"

"Look at the tiny dishes on the dining-room table!"

"The fireplace with little logs and a poker!"

"Look at the old-fashioned bath-tub!"

Amy stared. The grandfather doll was in the bedroom, and the grandmother was in the sitting-room, in the same positions in which she'd seen them last.

"You've moved the family around, Amy," Ellen said. "We had them in the dining-room, remember? Where's the girl doll? The one that's supposed to be your aunt?"

"She's in the box," Amy said tonelessly. "I just left them . . ." She stopped in confusion, but Ellen didn't ask any more questions.

The minutes dragged by while the girls looked into each room and found new details to admire. "We'd better go downstairs," Amy said finally, when it looked as if they would be content to stay there the rest of the evening. "You didn't finish telling my fortune, Cissie. You haven't done anybody's but Ellen's. And we're going to have birthday cake."

The girls got to their feet, except for Louise, who seemed hypnotized by the contents of the house.

"So little," she crooned. "So pretty." With a delicacy Amy wouldn't have thought possible, she reached into the sitting-room and picked up a tiny rocking chair with an embroidered seat. "So little," she said again. "I love the doll's house." She put the chair back and moved out of the way so Amy could close the front wall.

"Goodbye, house. Goodbye, dolls."

"Come on, Louise," Kathy urged. "You want your fortune told, don't you?"

They trooped downstairs, Ellen leading the way once more, and Amy, Louise and Kathy bringing up the rear.

"Goodbye, house," Louise called again. "Goodbye, dolls. I have to have my fortune told now."

Amy stopped for a last look at the sheeted house before following the others down the stairs. *It's just a toy,* she told herself. But she knew it was more than that. The moving dolls, the light—they were as real as the house itself. And since no one else knew about them, it was up to Amy to find out what they meant.

14.

"The Poor Dolly is Crying"

"Well, what do you think?" Aunt Clare stood with Amy, Louise, and Ellen on the front porch as the Sells' car pulled away. They waved and shouted good nights until the rear lights blinked out of sight around the curve and the stillness of the country night settled around them.

"A terrific party!" Amy said.

"It was really wonderful, Miss Treloar!" Ellen exclaimed. "After all, it had my two favourite things in the world—caramel popcorn and pizza! We had a great time."

"Was it all you wanted it to be, Amy?" asked Aunt Clare, as they turned back into the house. Aunt Clare glanced at Louise, who held a paper napkin filled, with the last of the caramel popcorn.

"It was perfect," Amy assured her. Except for those uncomfortable minutes in the attic, she'd loved the party. Having Louise there hadn't made any difference at all. Kathy had treated her the way she treated everyone else, and the other girls had followed suit. Aunt Clare had helped too, by keeping Louise busy when she threatened to take over the conversation, and by giving an occasional signal for her to calm down.

When the last dishes were stacked in the sink, Ellen yawned and stretched. "I'm really sleepy, all of a sudden," she said. "I'm going to bed to dream about the blond man coming into my life. Maybe it won't be the paper boy after all."

"What's wrong with the paper boy?" Amy demanded and yawned, too.

"He's ten years old." The girls went upstairs, giggling, while Aunt Clare lingered behind to check the doors and turn off the lights.

"You get up when you want to," she called after them. "You know where the breakfast things are, Amy. I'm not going to be in any great hurry to get moving tomorrow."

Amy felt as if she might fall asleep on her feet. She undressed quickly, called a last good-night to Ellen, and was dozing when Louise returned from the bathroom and climbed into the other side of the big bed.

"Good night, Amy."

"Good night."

"I like Kathy. She's my friend. She's going to take me to the museum sometime."

Amy burrowed into her pillow. "I can take you to the museum. I didn't know you wanted to go."

"Neither did I." Louise's voice started to fade. "Kathy says they have dolls at the museum. And doll's houses. I love doll's houses . . ."

She was asleep, her breathing deep and regular. Amy closed her eyes and tried to match her breathing to Louise's. *I'll take her to the library,* she thought. *We can look for books about doll's houses.* And then she was asleep, too.

The grandfather clock downstairs was striking two when Amy woke. Moonlight flooded the bedroom, as it had on Wednesday night when Aunt Clare had come to talk and had scared Amy half to death. What had awakened her this time? She sat up and stared at the door, expecting to see the knob turn again. After a breathless moment she turned to see if Louise was awake, too, and discovered that the other half of the bed was empty. Louise was gone.

Amy slid out of bed and listened. If Louise had gone down the hall to the bathroom, there was no point in following her and starting a conversation that would wake Ellen and Aunt Clare. But there was no sound of returning footsteps, and when Amy opened the door, the hall was dark and so was the bathroom.

She went to the top of the stairs. Could Louise have gone downstairs for a drink of water?

She should have woken me, Amy thought crossly. *I told her she should tell me if she had to get up.*

A sound, like a sigh, made her whirl and look down the shadowy hallway. The attic door was open—only a millimetre or two, but as Amy stared, she thought it opened farther. And she knew then, without a doubt, where her sister had gone.

"Darn, darn, darn!" Louise had awakened and decided to take another look at the doll's house in the middle of the night. She knew very well that Amy would have stopped her, so she had sneaked away by herself.

There was nothing to do but go to the attic after her. If Aunt Clare woke and heard someone moving around up there, she'd be frightened and angry. Amy had to get Louise back to bed without making a sound.

She tiptoed down the hall and slipped through the attic doorway. Moonlight made a silvery tunnel of the stairwell. If she was lucky, she'd be able to bring Louise back downstairs without switching on the light. *If I'm lucky,* she repeated to herself. *And if Louise doesn't see something that sends her into hysterics. If I don't have hysterics myself!*

Halfway up the steps, Amy began to feel as if she were reliving her nightmare visit to the attic twenty-four hours ago. There were the same noises—small, scratchy sounds, a little like a mouse might make, but not a mouse. Before she reached the top step, she saw that the house was open. The sitting-room was glowing eerily. In front of the house Louise knelt, staring with rapt attention into the lighted room.

Amy fought down the urge to run. She couldn't go without Louise. On tiptoe, she crossed the attic to her sister's side.

Louise looked up. "Look at the dolly," she said

in a voice that was much softer than usual.

Amy looked without wanting to. The grandmother doll still stood in front of the bookcase, but now one blue-clad arm was raised. As Amy stared, a tiny book fell from the shelf, and then another. And another. The simply slid off the shelves and lay scattered at the doll's feet.

"Books fall," Louise murmured. "The poor dolly is crying."

Amy gasped. A muted weeping had begun, a sound so despairing that it made her want to cry herself.

"That's not the doll crying," Amy whispered hoarsely. "Don't be silly." But the sobs were coming from the doll's house sitting-room.

"Louise, get up!" Amy couldn't fight back panic any longer. She tried to drag Louise to her feet. "We have to get out of here."

"Listen to the poor dolly, Amy. Why is she crying?"

"I don't know! *I don't know!*" Amy almost forgot to whisper. Clearly, Louise wasn't frightened at all; she rocked back on her heels as if she were watching a show and enjoying it. Perhaps that was what this was to her—a show like the puppet show at the mall. No more frightening, no more magical than that, and just as fascinating.

The light in the sitting-room began to fade. The sobbing stopped.

"Getting dark," Louise said. "Why, Amy?"

"I said I don't know. I don't know anything." This time Amy succeeded in getting Louise on her feet. "Walk on tiptoe," she ordered. "Aunt Clare will be angry with you if she finds out you came up here."

Looking only slightly worried, Louise started towards the stairs. Amy lingered a moment in front of the dark and silent house. Her heart pounded. The house *was* telling her something; in spite of her terror, she knew that. But what was it? Would she ever know?

With trembling fingers she closed and covered the house. "I'll try to work it out," she whispered and turned to follow Louise. From behind her, in the house, came the tiniest of sighs.

15.

"A Ghostly Secret"

Amy wasn't surprised to see Aunt Clare appear in the kitchen while the girls were eating breakfast. She was too energetic to stay in bed when everyone else was up.

"Have you had orange juice? There's tomato juice, too, if you'd rather. Or apricot? Amy, did you make plenty of toast?"

"We're fine. I thought you were going to sleep late this morning," Amy teased.

"I couldn't. I say I'm going to, but I always wake up early. On my last job"—Aunt Clare looked wistful—"I was up at six-thirty every morning to catch my train to work. On Saturdays and Sundays, when I could have slept late, I woke promptly at six-thirty just the same and stared at the ceiling for half an hour trying to convince myself I was enjoying the rest. I'm a morning person, and I might as well accept it. Have you had cereal?"

"And bananas. And orange marmelade. And strawberry and raspberry jam—" Amy was babbling. Ever since she got up, she'd been chattering, giggling, hurrying Louise, discussing the party with Ellen—anything to keep from thinking about what had happened in the attic last night.

Aunt Clare plugged in the coffee pot and put a slice of bread in the toaster. "What are you going to do this beautiful morning? Besides talk about who said what at the party, of course?"

"We're going for a hike to Rainbow Falls," Ellen replied eagerly. "We were going to bike there last Saturday, but my aunt and uncle came from Chicago."

"Good idea." Aunt Clare flicked a questioning glance at Louise, who was spreading a thick layer of jam on her toast.

"Louise is going with us." Amy felt rather than saw Ellen's look of surprise. "She likes to hike, don't you, Louise?"

"I like to hike," Louise agreed. "Or else, I want to go up and watch the poor dolly—"

"We'll take sandwiches," Amy said quickly. "What kind do you want, Louise?" She could hardly wait to get her sister out of the house. Louise knew she wasn't supposed to talk about the doll's house, but the temptation was too great.

"Peanut butter and pickles."

"Ellen?"

"Anything."

"Well, just take whatever you want." Aunt Clare sounded relieved that there were to be no arguments about what Louise would do. Later, when Ellen had gone upstairs to make the beds, taking Louise as a helper, Aunt Clare said, "Your friends are really very good with Louise."

"Not always." Amy busied herself slicing cheese and spreading peanut butter. "I've had friends who were really awful to her. She scares them, I guess. But Kathy Sells was terrific last night, and after a while everyone else copied the way she acted. Ellen, too, I guess. I still think Ellen backed out of our bike ride last Saturday because of Louise," she added.

"Then it's especially nice of you to take Louise along today," Aunt Clare said. "I hope it won't be a burden for you."

That word again! Amy wondered why it bothered her so much. After all, she'd certainly let Aunt Clare know Louise was a burden at the mall last Friday afternoon, *But she's my sister,* she wanted to say, *not just my burden.* She sighed. There was no easy way to explain her feelings. She couldn't even explain them to herself.

It wasn't until they were out of the house and walking down the country road that Amy relaxed. Warm sun pressed against her shoulders and the backs of her knees, and a breeze ruffled her hair. "This is great," she murmured. Now if Louise would just forget what happened last night. . . .

"The poor dolly cried," Louise announced. "The books fell down."

Louise never forgot anything—except warnings to keep quiet.

"What dolly? What books?" Ellen looked at Louise curiously.

"The dolly in the doll's house. She cried and cried."

Ellen turned to Amy. "Does she mean *the* doll's house?"

Amy nodded. Lying in bed that morning, before the others woke up, she'd realized that she probably wasn't going to be able to keep the secret of the doll's house to herself after all. Not now, with Louise knowing what she did. Besides, she really needed to talk about it to a friend. The whole thing was becoming too scary.

"Louise went up to the attic after we were all asleep last night," Amy said slowly. "I woke up and went after her." As briefly as possible, she described their adventure, then went on to tell Ellen about the strange events that had happened on previous nights. "I can't talk about it to Aunt Clare," she finished. "The doll's house really upsets her. She was furious when she thought I'd moved the dolls around to act out the murders." She shuddered. "As if I would."

"But you'll have to tell her," Ellen protested, eyes wide. "It's her doll's house, after all."

Amy shook her head. She reached for Louise's hand and drew her farther over on to the shoulder of the road. "She wouldn't believe me.

The thing is, I think the ghost"—she gulped over the word and hurried out—"is trying to tell us something. Something about the murders, maybe. And Aunt Clare doesn't want to think about them or talk about them. If I don't find out what the secret is, no one ever will."

"A ghostly secret!" Ellen's eyes shone. "Amy, that's the most exciting, most scary thing I've ever heard. I don't see how you could keep quiet about it. What are you going to do?"

"I don't know. This morning I thought about telling my dad, but he'd want to see for himself, and then Aunt Clare would know. She'd probably order us all out of the house."

"Maybe we should to back to the library and read some more about the murders."

Amy shrugged. "I have a feeling we wouldn't find out much. Maybe we can—" She was suddenly tired of thinking about a problem that seemed to have no answer. "Maybe we can just wait and see what happens—and today we can have a good time and forget about it. Come on! You, too, Louise! Race you to the park entrance."

Amy dashed ahead. In a moment Ellen had caught up with her, and she could hear Louise's heavier steps close behind. They all reached the park gate together.

"You're a good runner, Louise," Ellen panted as they slowed to a walk. "And you know something? You're the bravest person I know. I never would have gone up in that attic by myself in the middle of the night."

Louise looked puzzled. "Why not?" she asked earnestly.

"I wouldn't want to run into a ghost."

"I don't run into anything," Louise said smugly. "When I run, I just run." And away she went, leaning into the wind, leaving her companions far behind.

It was a perfect day for a picnic. The girls waded in the shallows of Rainbow River and sent sticks hurtling over the falls. They had their sandwiches on a flat rock overlooking the water, and in the afternoon they chased a cracked Frisbee Ellen found under a bush.

"Your sister is really fast," Ellen said. Louise continued throwing and pursuing the Frisbee after Amy and Ellen collapsed on the grass. "You know those Special Olympics—the ones for kids like Louise? She ought to be in that." Amy considered. "I don't think Mum would like that much."

"Why not? Louise would love it."

"She doesn't like to admit Louise is different." Amy wasn't in the mood to talk about that problem either.

"Our minister believes in ghosts," Ellen said after a few moments of silence.

"How do you know?"

"He said once—he said things happen that we can't explain. And if you see something like that, you should feel lucky, not afraid, because most people never have the experience. I'd be afraid," she added honestly.

"I bet he would, too," Amy said. "I bet he wouldn't feel so lucky up there in that attic with a ghost crying and lights going on and off and dolls moving. . ." She lay back, squinting into the sun. Grown-ups could make a lesson out of anything!

At three o'clock they gathered up their belongings, leaving the Frisbee on a picnic table for someone else to enjoy. Ellen's mother had said she would be at Aunt Clare's house at four.

"That was a good day!" Ellen exclaimed as they left the park. "When we moved to Claiborne, I didn't know anybody, and now I have a best friend. Just like Cissie said when she was telling my fortune. I'm glad it's you, Amy." She turned to Louise, who was listening intently. "You're a good friend, too, Louise."

Amy wished later that their day could have ended right there. But as they turned into the garden of the old house, they saw Aunt Clare sitting on the top step of the porch. Her face had a dark, closed-up look, and she barely nodded in response to the girls' hellos.

"Your mother called—she's on her way, Ellen," she said abruptly. "She wants you to be ready because she's in a hurry. Are you all packed?"

"Yes." Ellen looked at Amy.

"What's the matter, Aunt Clare?" Amy asked. "What's wrong?"

Her aunt glared at them. "I'm sure if you think about it, you'll know very well what's the matter. We'll talk later." Her voice shook with rage.

"I'll get my suitcase," Ellen said and hurried inside.

"But I *don't* know what's wrong," Amy insisted.

"We'll talk about it when Ellen is gone," Aunt Clare said tightly. "There's already been far too much talk in front of strangers."

They sat in silence on the steps until the crunch of tyres on gravel announced Mrs. Kramer's approach. Ellen must have been waiting and watching from an upstairs window, for as soon as the car turned into the garden, her footsteps sounded on the stairs. She came outside on tiptoe and closed the door gently behind her as if someone were ill.

"That you for the lovely party, Miss Treloar," she said. "It was really nice. See you Monday, Amy."

Amy nodded, too upset to speak.

"'Bye, Louise. 'Bye, everybody." Ellen jumped into the car and was gone.

"How dare you!" The words cut like a blade across the chirping, buzzing peace of late afternoon. Amy swung around to face her aunt. "How could you gossip about our family *to all those girls?* I can't forgive you for that, Amy. I told you how I felt about your putting the dolls in the rooms where they were murdered, and yet you went right up there and did it again last night. In front of everyone! You don't care how I feel!"

So that was it. Aunt Clare had been in the attic and looked into the doll's house.

"I went up to put Ellen's blanket away, and there was the house standing open the way you left it last night. And the dolls were in the bedroom and the sitting-room again! And the desk—oh, Amy, that was the worst! What were you doing—putting on a play for your friends? I just can't believe you'd be so insensitive."

"The desk?"

"You know what I'm talking about! The desk in the sitting-room was moved over in front of the door. You must have read about that when you and Ellen went poking through the newspapers, looking for all the grisly details. After Grandma Treloar ran downstairs to the sitting room with Paul, she pushed the desk against the door to try to keep the—killer out. It didn't stop him, but she tried. The desk is there in front of the sitting-room door now, right where you put it."

"I didn't!" Amy was suddenly angry, too. Aunt Clare had no right to assume she was guilty without giving her a chance to explain. "I didn't touch the dolls after we put them back in the box the other night. You were there and saw me do it. And I didn't touch the desk either."

Aunt Clare clenched her fists in exasperation. "Amy, this is terrible! Why must you lie to me?" You did move them—you or Ellen— there's no other explanation."

"Don't yell at Amy!" Louise was on her feet at the foot of the steps. "Amy doesn't lie. I don't like you!"

"And I don't like being lied to," Aunt Clare snapped. "Sit down, Louise. I'm talking to your sister."

"I saw the poor dolly," Louise shouted. "I heard the dolly cry."

"What in the world are you talking about?"

"The poor dolly—"

"Aunt Clare." Amy knew what she had to do. She struggled to keep her voice steady. "I didn't move the dolls when I was up there last week, and I didn't move them yesterday. Neither did Ellen. Something really strange is happening in the doll's house. The sitting-room lights up, all by itself, and the dolls move around. I saw the grandmother doll moving. I did!" She turned away from her aunt's disbelieving eyes and hurried on. "Last night Louise went up there after we were all asleep, and I went to look for her. The house was open again, and there was a light, and"—she took a deep breath—"there was crying coming from the sitting-room. And some of the little books fell off the shelves, all by themselves. I saw them!"

"The books fell down," Louise said in the silence that followed.

Amy waited for the explosion that was sure to follow her story. She hadn't wanted to tell, but Aunt Clare had forced her to do it. When the silence stretched out, she looked up and saw that Aunt Clare had buried her head in her arms. Her thin shoulders shook with sobs.

Amy scrambled up the steps and laid a timid hand on her aunt's arm. "I'm sorry. I didn't want to tell you. I wasn't ever going to tell you, because I knew you'd hate it. Please don't cry."

Aunt Clare didn't answer. Gradually her sobs became softer, but she didn't lift her head. She seemed to have forgotten Amy and Louise were there.

"Aunt Clare?"

"You'd better leave me alone for a while." The

words were muffled.

Amy signalled to Louise. "We'll be inside," she said. "Come on, Louise."

They were in the hall, looking at each other in bewilderment, when Aunt Clare spoke again. "I'd like to believe you wouldn't lie to me," she said tiredly. "But if you're telling the truth—if there's a restless, unhappy spirit haunting this place—that's even worse. Because it means what I've always suspected is true. And I can't bear *that*."

16.

"It Could Have Been Just Anyone"

The curtains on the west window were dancing in the wind when Amy and Louise entered their bedroom.

"There's going to be a storm," Amy said. She stood at the window and watched the clouds boiling up over the trees. The darkening sky matched her mood.

"Let's go home, Amy." Louise sagged against the foot of the bed. "I want to go home right now."

"We can't," Amy told her. "There's no one there."

"I don't care. I want to go now."

"I said we can't," Amy repeated. "Mum and Dad wouldn't like it if we stayed in the house alone overnight, and Aunt Clare would have a fit."

"She doesn't care." Louise stuck out her lower lip. "She doesn't like us. And I don't like her."

"Did Mum say anything about when she'd be back?" There was a slim chance her mother wouldn't wait for Dad's seminar to end on Sunday. After all, she'd only gone along so that Louise would have to be at Amy's party. Maybe she'd come home on the bus today.

"I don't remember," Louise said. "You call her and tell her to come right now."

Amy considered. "I could call and see if she's at our house, I suppose," she said. Amy was willing to try anything. She didn't want to stay another night any more than Louise did.

She tiptoed downstairs to the telephone, catching a glimpse of Aunt Clare still hunched on the top step of the porch. She looked like a little girl sitting there by herself. A *frightened* little girl.

Amy brushed away the thought. Aunt Clare knew as much about the haunted doll's house now as Amy did. If she refused to believe, whose fault was that? *She's not my responsibility any more.*

Amy let the telephone ring a dozen times, just in case her mother was in the basement or out in the garden. But she didn't really expect an answer. Her mother was almost certainly a hundred kilometres away in Madison shopping or having dinner with Dad.

"That isn't necessary." Amy whirled around. Aunt Clare stood on the other side of the screen door. "You don't have to call anyone. I don't want you to leave, Amy—not before we try to straighten this out." Her face was set and pale, but her voice was strong.

"We can't go home anyway," Amy said. "Nobody is there."

"Of course not." Aunt Clare came into the hall. "Let's go out in the kitchen and make some biscuits," she said. "I want to talk to you, and we might as well do something constructive at the same time. Where's Louise?"

"Upstairs in our bedroom."

"I upset her terribly, didn't I? And you. I'm sorry. Would you go up and ask her to come down? Tell her I've stopped roaring."

"She won't come—not until she feels like it." Amy followed her aunt to the kitchen, dizzied by her shift in mood and wondering what was going to happen next.

A flick of the light switch turned the kitchen into a cheery haven from the storm that was beginning to break overhead. "Chocolate chip?" Aunt Clare began getting out ingredients without waiting for an answer. Amy sank into a chair, still not sure what was expected of her.

I'm not going to talk about the doll's house, Aunt Clare said firmly. "I've thought it over, and I believe that you believe what you said is true. So it was wrong of me to say you lied. I hope you'll forgive me. My temper is my curse. But I do want you to know why I feel so strongly about being reminded of what happened in this house. The thing is, Amy"—she turned away to pour chocolate bits into a measuring cup—"I'm quite certain that it was my fiancé—Tom

Keaton—who murdered Grandpa and Grandma Treloar."

"Oh!" The word popped out of Amy as if she'd been hit in the stomach.

"Tom was eight years older—hotheaded, reckless, charming—exciting to a strong-willed eighteen-year-old girl who'd seen practically nothing of the world. Grandpa and Grandma met him only once—I told you about that—and they said I was to stop seeing him immediately. He was drunk when he came to the house. It seemed terribly unfair that they'd let one bad impression make up their minds and determine the course of my whole life. He'd already asked me to marry him by then, and I'd agreed."

"Oh, Aunt Clare—"

"Let me keep talking while I feel up to it," Aunt Clare hurried on. "You can get out the baking tins if you want. . .

"I was furious with Grandma and Grandpa. I told them a hundred, a thousand times that I didn't want to be treated like a child. I guess that's why I despised the doll's house. I was practically an adult when they gave it to me, and my grandmother insisted that it remain in my bedroom for the next three years. When I was a woman of eighteen, in love with an older man who said he loved me, I still had a doll's house in my bedroom!" Aunt Clare's voice shook. "It seems incredible now that a thing like that bothered me so much. But it did. I sulked and stormed all through those months, and I never stopped seeing Tom. Grandma and Grandpa suspected what I was doing, but they couldn't stop me. I'd pretend I was going out with other friends, and then I'd meet him somewhere. Or I'd just sneak out of the house after the others were asleep. Grandpa caught me coming in once, but he didn't tell Grandma. She wasn't well—she had severe arthritis—and he didn't want her to be any more upset than she already was."

Amy moved round the kitchen in a daze, setting the baking tins on the table, rinsing the measuring cups and spoons as Aunt Clare finished with them. At one point she realized Louise was standing in the doorway, watching and listening.

"Gradually I realized that Grandma and Grandpa might be right about Tom. He was drinking a great deal, and when he drank his temper was uncontrollable. Worse than mine! I was frightened, but I was far too stubborn to admit I was wrong about him. The more they tried to keep me at home—the more they treated me like a prisoner—the more determined I was to be with him. And then he began to insist that we get married soon. When I put him off, he blamed my grandparents for influencing me, and one afternoon he told me he was going to come to the house and have it out with them. I didn't believe him—he was drunk, rambling—I was sure it was just talk. That night I went to a film with girl friends, to have something else to think about. That was the night they were killed."

Later when Amy thought about Aunt Clare, she remembered watching teaspoonfuls of batter plop on to baking tins in neat rows. The familiar sound of the spoon scraping the bowl made Aunt Clare's words that much more horrifying.

"I came home from the cinema and found the front door standing open. The sitting-room door was partly closed and when I pushed it, something kept it from opening all the way. I peeked into the room and saw the desk—and I saw Grandma lying in front of the fireplace—blood. . . I ran upstairs, and Grandpa was lying across the bed in their room. Paul—Paul was nowhere! All I could think of was that Tom had come and killed them all. And it was my fault!"

"What did you do?" Amy's whisper was almost drowned out by a clap of thunder.

"I ran out of the house. The nearest neighbour was a kilometre away, but I never thought of using the phone. All I wanted was to run! When the police came, they found the phone lines had been cut, so I couldn't have called anyway."

Aunt Clare slid the biscuits into the oven. When she turned round, she saw Louise and motioned her to come in. "You're just in time, Louise. We'll have biscuits and milk in about ten minutes."

Louise, looking sullen, sat at the table and propped her chin on her hands. Amy sat next to her, and Aunt Clare pulled out a chair across from them.

"The police found Paul—your father—sound asleep in the wood cupboard in the sitting-room. He couldn't tell them a thing. They decided the killer must have broken in on Grandpa and Grandma in their bedroom. He shot Grandpa, and Grandma ran out of the room. She grabbed Paul from his bed and took him downstairs to the sitting-room. The phone lines were cut, and her arthritis was too bad for her to run away, so she did the only thing she could think of. She hid Paul in the cupboard, and then she pushed the desk up against the door as a barricade. But Tom—the killer—was too strong. He pushed the door open, and he killed her. Then he went through the house emptying drawers, pulling things out of cupboards, making a shambles."

Aunt Clare's voice faded, and for a few moments no one spoke. Then Amy suggested timidly, "Maybe it wasn't your fiancé who did it. If things were stolen, it could have been just anyone. A burglar—"

"Tom would have been clever enough to make it look like a burglary," Aunt Clare said. "And I know he owned a gun. I don't think he came here meaning to kill them—he probably intended to frighten them. But when he suddenly appeared in their bedroom, they must have told him exactly what they thought of him. Grandma would have, I'm sure. And he went crazy! I've imagined it a thousand times, every hideous minute of it. Sometimes I feel as if I were there myself."

She sighed, looking into the girls' white faces. "I'm talking too much," she said. "But I want you to know how it was. . . . Later, the next day—the house was full of policemen and my grandparents' friends—I realized that some thing *else* was wrong. People were looking at me and whispering. Finally someone told me that there'd been a car accident, and Tom was dead. He'd been driving at high speed on a road north of the town, and he'd hit a tree. No one knew we were engaged—I'd never dared announce it—but there'd been rumours, and everyone knew we were close. I suppose the police wondered if there could be a connection between the two tragedies, but Tom had friends who testified that he'd been with them all evening. So that was it. The police called it 'murder by person or persons unknown'. And I was the only person who guessed the truth."

The timer buzzed, and Amy and Louise jumped. Aunt Clare got up and opened the oven. "Perfect," she said. "There's something soothing about baking. It's one thing you can count on to turn out right, if you just follow directions."

She lifted the trays from the oven and set them on trivets to cool. Then she went to the refrigerator and poured tall glasses of milk.

"As soon as I could get away—as soon as I knew Paul would be taken care of—I went to Chicago to look for a job. I never wanted to see Claiborne or be reminded of what happened here again."

"But you did come back," Amy marvelled. "I don't think I could have done it."

"I didn't have much choice," Aunt Clare replied. "You see, even though I'd left Claiborne behind, I couldn't forget. The guilt—the terrible feeling that Grandma and Grandpa died because of me—just about drove me out of my mind. Eventually I found a good job, but six months later I was fired. I had awful headaches that made me miss work—and moody times when I just couldn't get control of myself. I found another job, and the same thing happened. It's never really stopped. The periods between 'explosions' are longer now, but the bad times haven't ended. I dream again and again about this house and what happened here. A couple of months ago, after a long period of sleeplessness, I had a battle with my boss—and I was out of a job again. Just about then, your father wrote, pleading with me to take time to look over the house and get it ready to be sold. I had nowhere else to go, nothing else to do. I thought maybe if I came back and emptied the old place of its memories, I'd be able to make a fresh start."

She loosened the biscuits with a spatula, transferring them one at a time to a plate. "So here I am," she said dryly, "scaring my two nieces to death with all the gruesome details I wanted to forget—and with a haunted doll's house, so you tell me, up in the attic. That's a thought I can't tolerate—the idea that my grandparents can't rest peacefully, any more than I can." She smiled wearily at Amy.

Louise bit into a biscuit. "Yum," she said, smacking her lips. "You make good biscuits, Aunt Clare. I guess we can stay here tonight."

Aunt Clare laughed. She touched Louise lightly on the top of the head. "Thanks," she said. "I needed that."

The telephone rang, and Amy jumped up to answer it. She welcomed a moment away from the kitchen. *It's so sad,* she thought, forgetting how angry she'd been with Aunt Clare half an hour earlier. *No wonder she's moody and bad-tempered sometimes. That horrible night has spoiled her whole life.*

Amy's mother was on the phone. "I'm still in Sun Prairie, Amy," she said. She sounded tired. "It's been a difficult twenty-four hours here. John is terribly ill but the doctors are more encouraging now that they were last night."

"John?" Amy felt as if she were coming back from a great distance. John was Barbara's husband. And he really was sick? Her mother hadn't made up the emergency after all?

"He had an operation late last night," her mother said. "Barbara's practically in shock."

"That's awful," Amy said. "I hope he'll be all right."

"So do I. Oh, Amy," her mother's voice warmed, "I'n sorry about last night—I really am. I know you wanted your party to be all your own, so for me to thrust Louise on you and Clare. . . but there was no other way. Barbara has two tiny children, and they've kept me busy while she's been at the hospital with John."

Amy felt as if she should apologize to her mother, but she didn't. "We had a great time last night," she said, knowing that would make her mother feel better than anything else she could say. "Louise was fine. It was a really good party."

"That's wonderful!" The tired note was gone. "I can't tell you how relieved I am."

"When will you be home?"

"I just talked to your father on the phone. Barbara's mother expects to get here tomorrow afternoon from California, and she'll take over with the children. Unless something unexpected happens before then, Dad and I'll be back tomorrow night." Her mother paused. "How about you?"

"How about me what?" Amy was confused.

"When will you be home to stay?"

Right away! Amy wanted to shout it into the phone. She thought of sitting at the dinner table with her own family, of going to bed in her own bedroom.

"I don't know," she said. And then, "Soon."

It was the best she could do. She knew her mother was disappointed. But she couldn't leave now, right after Aunt Clare had confided in them. More than ever, she had to uncover the secret of the doll's house. If there was a secret at all.

17.

"Someone's Walking on the Doll's House Stairs"

The storm centred over the house. A brilliant flash of lightning brought Amy straight up in bed, just as the first raindrops thudded on the roof.

"Ameee!" Louise's panicky cry was muffled by the sheet. She had pulled it over her head and was curled up into a tight ball. "Ameee!"

The big bed shuddered under the crash of thunder. "There's nothing to be afraid of." Amy tried to sound calm.

"There is, too." But Louise sounded as if she were strangling. "It's worse than the thunder at our house, Amy."

"No, it isn't." But Louise was right. At home, other people and houses were close by; here in the country, the house stood by itself. *As if tonight wasn't going to be scary enough without a storm!* Amy thought.

She'd been awake for an hour, thinking about what she had to do. The doll's house was trying to tell her something. She didn't want to go up to the attic again, but she knew she must.

"Don't go to sleep, Louise," Amy whispered. "We're going to do something in a few minutes—as soon as Aunt Clare's had time to fall asleep."

The sheet was lowered slightly, and in the next flash of lightning, Amy saw Louise peering out at her. "I can't go to sleep when I'm afraid," she said. "What're we going to do?"

"We're going up to the attic to look at the doll's house. Watch it. See if anything else happens."

"No." The sheet went back up.

"Why not?"

"Thunder. I don't like the thunder, Amy." There was another breathtaking clap, and Louise moaned.

Amy was disappointed. She'd been counting on her sister's company; it would help to be with someone who wasn't afraid of dolls that moved and a doll's house that lighted up by itself. But if Louise was going to scream every time there was a crash of thunder, she'd be no comfort at all.

Amy slipped out of bed and opened the bedroom door a crack. Aunt Clare's door was tightly closed.

"Is Aunt Clare sleeping?" Louise was peeking again. "I guess so. She said she didn't feel tired, so she was going to take a sleeping pill. It must have worked by now." Amy found her slippers under the bed and put them on. "I'm going up to the attic, Louise. You stay under the covers and keep your eyes closed tight, the way you do at home. You'll be all right."

There was a subdued sniffle. Then the mound of bed covers erupted. "I'll go with you."

"You don't have to. The thunder will sound louder up there."

"That's all right." Louise slid out of bed and reached for Amy's hand. "I want to be with you."

Amy felt better. She led the way down the hall as lightning leaped across the window at the far end and thunder rattled the panes. Louise trembled.

When they opened the attic door, the darkness was daunting.

"Too black," Louise whimpered. "Turn on the light, Amy."

Amy drew her into the stairwell. "The lightning will help us see," she whispered. "We want it to be dark—if the light comes on in the doll's house, we want to see it happen."

As they climbed the stairs, Amy listened for other sounds between thunderclaps—the small scratchy noise of dolls moving about. When they reached the top step, lightning lit the attic. The doll's house stood open.

"Walk on tiptoe," Amy ordered. "And don't talk out loud—whatever happens. Aunt Clare mustn't wake up."

"All right." Louise tightened her grip on Amy's hand and let herself be led across the attic to the corner. The girls knelt in front of the open doll's house.

They waited while the rain beat a wild tattoo over their heads. The lightning flashes grew farther apart, but the thunder was as loud as ever. After what seemed an endless time Amy shifted her weight; one foot was starting to tingle. Almost imperceptibly, the doll's house sitting-room became easier to see. "It's starting!" Amy whispered. She could make out the furniture in the little room, the high-backed sofa and chairs, the desk set firmly against the closed door. The grandmother doll stood facing the bookshelves as before, her arm upraised.

"Poor dolly," Louise murmured, hearing what Amy had missed at first because of the rain. The crying again! It came from the sitting-room—soft, racking sobs. Then the grand-mother doll tipped forward, until one tiny china hand rested on a book on the shelf.

Amy gasped. Until this moment, a part of her had insisted that the haunting of the doll's house *could* be a product of her imagination. She *thought* she'd seen the dolls move before; she *thought* they were able to move by themselves. But now she was sitting in front of the sitting room watching it happen.

"Amy?" Louise looked over her shoulder. "Someone's coming up the steps."

Amy turned. "Aunt Clare, is that you!" She hardly recognised her own quavering voice. "Aunt Clare?"

The footsteps continued. Heavy. Shuffling. Skinny, quick-stepping Aunt Clare had never walked like that.

"Amy, it's in the doll's house,"Louise said wonderingly. "Someone's walking on the doll's house stairs." She leaned forward, her head cocked in puzzlement. "Someone's coming down the doll's house stairs. But I can't see anyone."

Amy threw an arm round her sister. The footsteps stopped, and the sobbing grew louder, more frantic. The doll at the bookcase pivoted slowly, just as something heavy thudded against the sitting-room door.

"Oh, no!" Amy struggled to get up, but she couldn't. Her legs wouldn't hold her. Her mind was a blur. She'd come to the attic to learn the secret of the doll's house, but she didn't want to see this. Not a murder!

The sobbing was all around them now. The sitting-room door shook under the impact of the invisible attacker. Louise jumped up.

"Let's go, Amy. I don't want to stay here anymore."

There was a final thud, louder than all the others. The sitting-room door burst open, shoving the desk to one side. A high, thin scream filled the attic.

Amy stared at the gaping door and at the grandmother doll pressing back against the bookshelves. Panic gave her strength, and she scrambled to her feet. The girls dashed across the attic and down the stairs. As they threw open the door at the bottom and tumbled into the hall, a roll of thunder set the whole house trembling.

"Aunt Clare!" Amy shrieked. Louise shouted, "Mummy!" And they hurtled into their aunt's bedroom as if the killer himself were right behind them.

18.

"More Ghosts, Amy?"

"What in the world!" Aunt Clare sounded stunned. Lightning filled the room with blue light as she blinked at the figures clutching each other at the foot of her bed. "Who's there? What's happened?"

"In the attic—we s-saw—" Thunder drowned out Amy's stammer.

Aunt Clare flicked on a lamp and swung her feet over the side of the bed. "Wait a minute," she commanded, though with not quite her usual vigour. The pill had put her to sleep in spite of the storm, and obviously she was having difficulty waking up now. "Do you mean you've been in the attic again?"

"We had to!" Amy saw her aunt's lips tighten. "We did it for you, Aunt Clare. Don't be angry.

We saw—*we saw*-" But the words wouldn't come.

Aunt Clare reached for her gown. "I'm not angry, Amy—I just don't understand what you're trying to tell me. Good grief, what a storm! Let's go downstairs. Maybe I can hear you better down there."

Meekly the girls followed along the hall to the stairs. Amy darted a glance at the attic door; it was closed. *I wouldn't go up there again,* she thought, *for all the secrets in the world.*

Lightning lit their way and thunder bombarded them as they trailed into the kitchen. "I'll make cocoa," Aunt Clare said. "It'll calm you down." She combined chocolate, sugar, and milk, while the girls huddled near the door. "You may have noticed I'm a firm believer in the soothing powers of a snack. Though, of course, doctors don't approve of using food for comfort. In my experience, chocolate never fails. Chocolate-chip biscuits are very useful. Also fudge. And cocoa." She kept glancing at the girls as she chattered. "I'll pull the blinds if you like—the storm makes things seem much worse than they are. . ."

The words flowed over and around Amy. *If my legs would only stop shaking,* she thought. *If my chest didn't feel so funny and tight. . . .*

Aunt Clare gave up the attempt at conversation. "You'd both better sit down before you fall down," she suggested.

Amy moved towards the table and Louise followed. Just then another clap of thunder crashed over them rattling dishes in the cupboards. The room was plunged into darkness, and Louise squealed in terror.

"Damn!" They could hear Aunt Clare moving across the kitchen. "Stay where you are, children. There's an oil lamp on the top shelf of the cupboard. I'll have it in a minute."

Amy couldn't have taken a step if she'd wanted to. With the lights out, the terror she'd felt in the attic returned full force. Beside her, Louise sobbed, her panic increasing with each clap of thunder. Amy put an arm round her sister's shoulders and drew her close.

"There now." A match flared, and yellow light brightened the kitchen. Aunt Clare turned up the flame of the lamp. "That's cozy, isn't it?" She lifted the pot from the stove and poured the cocoa into mugs. "Come on, don't cry, Louise. Have a nice hot drink and tell me what it was that scared you so. More ghosts, Amy?"

The question was lightly put, but Amy heard the tension behind it. They were back to a dangerous subject again. There was no escaping it.

Amy sipped her cocoa and tried not to look into the shadows beyond the lamplight. "We saw a doll move," she began cautiously. "All by itself. And we heard things, too." When her aunt didn't stop her, she described what had happened in the attic a few minutes earlier.

Aunt Clare regarded her solemnly. "You're sure, Amy? You couldn't have imagined the crying, the footsteps?"

"Oh, *no!*"

"You heard it, too, Louise?"

"And there was thunder all the time," Louise said, clearly feeling Amy had left out something important. "Just like now." For her, the storm remained the most frightening part of the night.

Aunt Clare leaned forward and rested her chin on her hands. Her face was gaunt. "Then it's true," she said finally. "There's really something up there—angry and full of hate, after all these years."

Amy squirmed. "What do you mean?"

"If there's a spirit haunting this place," Aunt Clare spoke slowly, "I'm sure it's Grandma Treloar's. She was the strong one, the one who hated Tom so much and despised me for loving him. Now she wants to make me suffer because I brought him into their lives . . . and caused their deaths." Her voice broke.

"Maybe not," Amy protested. "Maybe that isn't it." But she thought Aunt Clare was probably right. "It could be—it could be that the ghost wants to tell us something else—something about the books in the sitting-room," she went on, the idea taking shape as she spoke. "Last night the grandmother doll was there in the sitting-room, and the books started sliding out of the shelves. We didn't understand what that meant, and so—so tonight she leaned forward and touched them—first one and then another. Do you think maybe—"

She and Aunt Clare stared at each other, wide-eyed. Aunt Clare stood and picked up the lamp. "We can find out," she said grimly. "I may regret it, but we have to look, don't we?"

"Look at what?" Louise clutched her cocoa mug.

"The books in the sitting-room," Amy explained. "Maybe Grandma Treloar's spirit was using the doll to tell us there's something hidden behind the books. Come on, Louise. We'll close the curtains in the sitting-room so you can't see the lightning."

Reluctantly, Louise stood up. The little procession made its way down the hall, Aunt Clare leading the way with the lamp. Amy shivered as they entered the sitting-room. There was a chilling dampness that she'd never noticed before.

Aunt Clare set the lamp on a table and went from window to window, closing the velvet curtains. Then she pointed to the bookshelves. "Amy, you stand in front of the shelves and put up your hand the way the doll did in the doll's house. Grandma Treloar wasn't very tall . . . ." Her voice shook. "I can't believe we're doing this. People would think we're absolutely insane."

Amy loosened Louise's grip on her arm and positioned herself in front of the shelves. She was still terrified, but for the first time she felt as if she might be close to learning the secret of the haunted doll's house. She raised her hand and ran her fingertips over a row of books.

"Take them out, one or two at a time," Aunt Clare suggested. "There *could* be something behind them, I suppose. I'm sure those books haven't been touched in thirty years."

Amy pulled out four books, and sneezed as a cloud of dust drifted down over her head. She slid a hand into the empty space they left.

"Nothing," she reported.

Aunt Clare put the books on the table. "Take out some more, then. Let's empty that shelf and the one above it."

Amy pulled out another handful of books, and then another. She emptied the first shelf and started on the second. The table filled up, and Louise carried some of the books to the sofa.

"Let's stop for a while and look through these," Aunt Clare said. Her face was so white that she looked like a ghost herself. "There might be something tucked between the pages, I suppose . . . Oh, I feel ridiculous—and afraid of what we *might* find!"

Louise gathered up more books from the table just as a tremendous thunderclap broke overhead. The books flew out of her hands, and she sank to the floor. "Make it go away," she moaned. "Make it stop, Amy."

"I can't." Amy knew Louise was trying hard to be brave. At home, she often became hysterical during severe thunderstorms. "Come on, pick up the books, Louise. You're a good helper."

Louise rubbed her eyes with her fists and did as she was told. "Books, books, books," she muttered. "Books all over the floor. Books and a letter."

"A letter?" Amy turned from the bookcase. Her sister was looking at a sheet of paper with irritation.

"It was in a book," Louise said. "It fell out. I didn't do it."

Amy snatched the paper from Louise's fingers and held it close to the lamp.

"A bookmark, maybe?" Aunt Clare suggested. She leaned across the table for a better look, then straightened up with a gasp. "That's Grandma Treloar's handwriting. I'd know it anywhere. Oh, Amy!" She closed her eyes and turned away. "You read it, please. I can't bear to."

Amy's hand trembled so much that she could hardly make out the words scrawled on the paper. " 'He killed James,' " she read huskily. " 'He wants money. He's going to kill me, too. We've always been generous to Reuben—how could he do this? Please, God, don't let Paul wake up—' "

That was all. Amy looked up at her aunt, who clung to the edge of the table as if she might faint. "Who's Reuben?"

Aunt Clare cleared her throat. "Let me see the note, Amy. Please." She held the paper close to the lamp and read it again. "Reuben Miller was the handyman who took care of the garden and did chores around the house," she said. "He worked for a number of other people, too. He was quiet—serious—very de-dependable." She began to cry. "*Reuben Miller!* Oh, Amy, I know the police questioned him at the time, but he seemed so outraged by the killings, and his wife swore he was at home that evening. . . ."

"Where is he now?"

"He died, long ago," Aunt Clare dropped into a chair and leaned back. "I just can't take it in. So you see what this means? Tom didn't kill Grandma and Grandad. It wasn't my fault they died!"

Amy watched her aunt study the message again.

Something magic was happening, a small miracle in the circle of yellow lamplight. Tight little lines in Aunt Clare's face melted away, and her pale cheeks flushed with colour. She looked, younger, gentler, prettier than Amy had ever seen her before.

"When you said there was a ghost, I was angry with you, Amy," she murmured. "I thought, if that's true, the ghost is Grandma Treloar, and she's still furious after all these years because her killer was never identified. I thought, she wants me to go on feeling guilty forever! But now I know Tom didn't kill them. And Grandma Treloar wanted me to know the truth. If her spirit has come back, it's because she wants me to stop driving myself crazy over something that wasn't my fault at all." She was like a little girl, thrilled and relieved, asking Amy and Louise to be happy with her. "Don't *you* think that's why she came back?"

"*I* think the thunder is stopping," Louise replied. "That's what I think." She turned from Aunt Clare to Amy as they burst out laughing. "Not funny," she scolded. "The thunder was bad."

The electricity came back on as they returned to the kitchen. In the bright light, Aunt Clare read Grandma Treloar's note still another time. When she put it down at last, Louise picked it up from the table and slipped it inside a book she'd brought with her from the sitting room.

"It belongs here in this book," she said primly. "This is the book it fell out of." She laid the thin volume on the table with a satisfied air.

Amy stared at the book and then at Aunt Clare.

"I can't believe it," Aunt Clare said, shaking her head. "It's just a wild coincidence. Grandma must have grabbed the first book she touched."

Amy nodded. After all, everything about this night had been hard to believe. But she picked up the book and ran her fingers across the cover.

A Play by Henrik Ibsen, it said across the top of the binding, and then in large letters the title: *A Doll's House.*

19.

"Like a Real Family"

The morning was washed fresh by the storm of
the night before. Aunt Clare drifted around the
house with a smile on her face. She hummed as
they dressed for church and was thoughtful on
the drive home after the service.

"I feel so *light*," she marvelled. "As if a whole
world has slipped off my shoulders. I can't tell
you how different I feel!"

Amy thought she knew. Aunt Clare didn't
need her anymore; there was a new serenity in
her aunts's manner and in the old house itself.
And that was good, because Amy was ready to
go home. She was grateful that Aunt Clare
didn't protest when she said she and Louise
would leave as soon as their parents came back.

"I do want your father to know about Reuben

Miller," Aunt Clare said. "He has a right to hear the truth. But I'm not going to tell him or anyone else how we happened to discover Grandma Treloar's note. If you want to tell, it's up to you. I still can hardly believe it myself. If your father thinks I should tell the police about Reuben, I will, though I doubt anyone cares anymore who did the killings—anyone but me, that is."

"I'm going to tell Ellen everything," Amy said. "*She'll* believe it." A long, wonderful summer lay ahead, with a best friend she could really talk to.

Aunt Clare nodded. "Ellen's a good friend. You know," she said suddenly, "I think I'm going to enjoy my own friends more when I get back to Chicago. It'll be different this time, because I'll be different. No more nightmares about Grandma and Grandpa despising me, blaming me. No more guilty feelings—though I'll always be sorry I gave them such a hard time. I'm going to find a job I like, and just start over." She leaned across the table earnestly. "I'd like you to be as carefree as I am at this moment, Amy. You're like a daughter to me."

Her glance touched on Louise, and Amy knew what she was thinking about. They sat quietly, deep in their separate thoughts, until Louise grew bored and wandered upstairs. She had a box of treasures to examine—some old games Aunt Clare had found in the back of a cupboard. Her heavy tread echoed on the stairs.

"I keep thinking about what brought you here a week ago," Aunt Clare said. "How frustrated you were. What are you going to do the next time you feel like running?" It was the same question Amy had asked herself.

"I know your mother doesn't want any more advice from me," Aunt Clare went on. "But maybe you and she can talk things over one of these days. You can help her to understand that you and Louise must have time apart occasionally. You need it, and Louise has a right to meet other people—"

"Like Mrs. Peck." Amy remembered her jealous twinges when Louise talked about the fun she and Marisa had been having.

"Like Mrs. Peck," Aunt Clare agreed. "It would be great if Louise could go on spending time with her all summer. Just because you're on holiday, you shouldn't become a full-time sister-sitter."

"Mum thinks we should take care of Louise ourselves." Amy picked her words carefully. She'd never tried to explain this to anyone else before—or to herself. "I suppose I think we should, too, even though I get awfully tired of it. I don't know why, but that's how it is."

Aunt Clare began gathering the plates and glasses. "I'll say one thing more, and then I'll be quiet." She grinned at Amy. "I may not have experience raising children, but I *am* an expert on guilt feelings. And I'm pretty sure your mother feels as guilty in her way as I do in mine. She blames herself because Louise is brain-damaged—there isn't any reason for her to do that, but it's a perfectly human way to feel. And because she feels guilty, you and your father feel guilty, too. Louise is *your* family burden, and it's up to your family to take care of her—isn't that the way you look at it?"

Amy was astonished. She had never thought that her mother might feel responsible for Louise being the way she was. It was possible, she supposed. Still, there was something wrong with Aunt Clare's description of their feelings . . . . something missing. She wanted to talk about it some more, but the sound of a car on the gravel cut short the discussion.

"Mum and Dad are here!" Louise pounded down the stairs and ran outside. Moments later, they were all on the front porch, hugging each other as if they'd been apart for weeks.

"Happy late birthday!" Amy's father exclaimed. "It's an awful responsibility, having a teenager in the family. Makes me feel older myself."

Amy made a face at him. "How's Barbara's husband?" she asked. "Is he going to be all right?"

Her mother's face clouded. "The doctors still don't know if he'll recover. I feel so sorry for that little family." She hugged Amy and Louise again. "I just couldn't wait to get back to see you both. We're so lucky . . . ."

Aunt Clare left them on the porch together while she went inside to pour lemonade and fill a plate with biscuits.

"We're both going home with you today," Amy said shyly. "I've got my stuff all packed."

Her mother looked delighted. "I'm glad! We've missed you, Amy—especially Louise."

"Why 'especially Louise'?" Mr. Treloar demanded. "I missed Amy as much as anybody."

"I missed Amy as much as anybody," Louise repeated. "Aunt Clare gave me games," she said, changing the subject. "I know how to play them. Amy says I don't, but I do."

"You do not," Amy argued. "I told you this morning, you have to throw dice and then move—"

"I know how. I do!" Suddenly Louise's face was flushed. She scrambled across the porch on all fours and leaned against her mother's knees. "Tell Amy I know how," she commanded. "You tell her, Mum."

"Amy, please don't get her upset . . . ."

It was a scene they had played many times before. But this time there was a difference and Amy knew it, even as she glared at Louise. In the last two days and nights, she and her sister had been through a lot together. They'd been partners, holding on to each other when they were too frightened to stand alone. At that moment Amy knew what Aunt Clare had left out when she talked about "your family burden." She'd left out love. Louise, crouched there like a small child, full of resentment and frustration, was a real person. A sister. She'd been brave when Amy was afraid. She had good points and bad points like everyone else.

"I'll play the games with you next week, Louise," Amy offered. "Or maybe Mrs. Peck will. If I'm busy doing something else." She looked into her mother's eyes as she said that, and waited, not breathing, for the nod that finally came.

"Sounds like a fine arrangement to me," her father said. "And that lemonade looks terrific, Clare." He opened the screen door for Aunt Clare, who had been standing there with a tray of glasses, not wanting to interrupt. Louise scrambled up, her anger forgotten, and handed the glasses around.

"There's nothing like a snack," she announced, in a voice so much like Aunt Clare's that they all laughed.

An hour passed. The Treloars lingered on the porch, sipping their drinks and listening to Aunt Clare's plans for closing up the house and returning to Chicago. At last Amy's father put down his glass and stood up.

"We'd better head for home," he said. "It's been a long hard weekend."

For all of us, Amy thought.

Aunt Clare jumped to her feet. "Before you leave, there's something I want you to see in the attic, Paul," she said. "I'm sure you've forgotten it exists—you were so small when I got it."

Amy felt a familiar sinking in the pit of her stomach. She didn't want to go up to the attic again. She just wanted to go home. But when the others filed into the house after Aunt Clare, she couldn't very well stay behind.

Louise raced ahead when they reached the attic door. "This way," she shouted. "I know what it is."

The doll's house stood open, just as they'd left

149

it the night before. No, not quite. Amy felt goose bumps on her arms. The dolls had moved again. All four—the grandmother and grandfather, the big sister and the little boy—were seated at the dining room table, the way she and Ellen had arranged them more than a week ago. Amy glanced sideways at Aunt Clare, and saw her aunt's eyes widen.

"Why, this is gorgeous!" Mrs. Treloar exclaimed. "Clare, it's the loveliest doll's house I've ever seen. Wherever did it come from?"

"It was mine when I was a girl. But it's never been played with, and I think that's too bad. Somehow—" Aunt Clare smiled teasingly at Amy—"somehow I don't think Amy would enjoy it much, even though she likes miniatures. But I know Louise would. I'd like her to have it."

Mrs. Treloar was astounded. "Oh, it's much too valuable!" she exclaimed. "It belongs in a museum. Louise might break things. You mustn't—"

Her protest faded as Louise dropped to her knees and reached into the house to touch a table, then a chair, with a gentle finger.

"Mine?" she asked in an incredulous whisper. "The doll's house is *mine?*"

"It certainly is," Aunt Clare said. "If your mother and father say it's all right."

Amy's father cleared his throat. "I'm sure Louise will take very good care of it," he said. There were tears in his eyes, and for a moment Amy thought of what it must have been like for him on that long-ago night—awakened by police in the dark wood cupboard, and carried off to live with strangers. He had his own terrible memories to live with.

Now he was looking at the dolls gathered around the table. "They seem happy, don't they?" he said. "Like a real family." He put an arm around Amy and rested his other hand on Louise's shoulder. "Best thing in the world—a family," he said. "Agreed, Amy?"

Amy leaned against him. "Agreed," she said. "Agreed, Louise?"

But Louise was too busy to answer. She was passing a tiny china plate from one doll to another. "Have a chocolate-chip biscuit," she coaxed. "You'll feel much better."